Judson had to get Addie out of the direct line of fire.

Of course, a bullet could still reach her, but it would make the shooter's job much harder.

Judson used his body to muscle hers beneath the cruiser.

He tore his gaze from hers. Had to. And Judson also had to shove aside the hurricane of emotions roaring through him.

The fury over the attempts to kill them.

The danger the gunman had brought right to the ranch's doorstep, putting the babies in harm's way yet again.

Yes, he had to put all of that aside and try drowning out everything but the way the barrage of shots was slamming into the porch and cruiser.

TEXAS BABY RESCUE

DELORES FOSSEN

MIX
Paper | Supporting responsible forestry
FSC® C021394

Recycling programs for this product may not exist in your area.

ISBN-13: 978-1-335-69042-5

Texas Baby Rescue

For questions and comments about the quality of this book, please contact us at CustomerService@Harlequin.com.

Harlequin Enterprises ULC
22 Adelaide St. West, 41st Floor
Toronto, Ontario M5H 4E3, Canada
www.Harlequin.com

HarperCollins Publishers
Macken House, 39/40 Mayor Street Upper,
Dublin 1, D01 C9W8, Ireland
www.HarperCollins.com

Printed in Lithuania

Delores Fossen, a *USA TODAY* bestselling author, has written over a hundred and fifty novels, with millions of copies of her books in print worldwide. She's received a Booksellers' Best Award and an RT Reviewers' Choice Best Book Award. She was also a finalist for a prestigious RITA® Award. You can contact the author through her website at www.deloresfossen.com.

Books by Delores Fossen

Harlequin Intrigue

Renegade Canyon

Her Baby, Her Badge
Deputies Under Fire
Texas Baby Rescue

Saddle Ridge Justice

The Sheriff's Baby
Protecting the Newborn
Tracking Down the Lawman's Son
Child in Jeopardy

Silver Creek Lawman: Second Generation

Targeted in Silver Creek
Maverick Detective Dad
Last Seen in Silver Creek
Marked for Revenge

The Law in Lubbock County

Sheriff in the Saddle
Maverick Justice
Lawman to the Core
Spurred to Justice

Visit the Author Profile page at Harlequin.com.

CAST OF CHARACTERS

Deputy Judson Docherty—When orphaned twin newborns Lily and Rose are taken from a local foster care ranch in their small Texas town, Judson teams up with his ex in a desperate search to find them before it's too late.

Addie Jansen—Foster mother and current manager of the Horseshoe Ranch. Even though Judson and she share a painful past, she puts all of that aside to help locate the babies.

Yvette O'Dell—She lost custody of her own twins over twenty years ago, and they were sent to the Horseshoe Ranch. Now, she's the primary suspect in Lily and Rose's abduction.

Trevor Cates—Yvette's husband. Many believe he could have coerced Yvette into taking the babies. But why?

Jennifer Rankin—Yvette's biological now grown daughter, who could have her own agenda for wanting Lily and Rose.

Shane Rankin—Yvette's biological son. He perhaps orchestrated the abduction as a way to get his hands on his mother's estate.

Elijah Banks—Jennifer's fiancé, who's at odds with everyone in Jennifer's family. Did he have some involvement in taking the twins, or is he the abductor's scapegoat?

Chapter One

The cribs were empty.

That was the first thing Deputy Judson Docherty noticed when he hurried into the nursery of the Horseshoe Ranch. Even though he had been expecting the empty cribs because of the warning that he'd gotten during the phone call, it was still a jolt to realize the caller had been right.

Get here fast. The babies are missing.

That call had come ten minutes earlier, just as Judson had been heading home after a long shift at Renegade Canyon Sheriff's Office, and the caller, Addie Jansen, hadn't stayed on the line. After blurting out that dire announcement, she had hung up on him, no doubt to do a frantic search for the babies.

But where the hell was Addie now?

Judson hadn't seen her when he'd driven up to the ranch. Nor when he'd bolted inside through the already-open door of the house. And she hadn't responded the multiple times he'd called out for her.

Pushing aside that something really bad had happened to Addie and the babies, he raced through the sprawling house that was normally filled with the sounds of foster kids. Lots of them.

But tonight, there was nothing.

It was eerily quiet, and that was in part due to there being only two babies currently in care here, six-week-old twin girls Lily and Rose Alcott. But Addie and at least one of her helpers should have been around.

"Addie?" he called out again.

And this time, Judson thankfully got a response. It hadn't come from Addie, though.

"Out here," someone shouted, and silver-haired Etta Jean Milford stuck her head in through the back door.

Judson had known Etta Jean most of his life, since she had been the cook and caretaker way back when he'd been a foster kid at the ranch, nearly thirty years ago. And even though she was now in her late sixties, she was still going strong and usually looked as steady a proverbial rock. But not at the moment. Her face was tight with worry and barely controlled panic.

"The babies aren't here," the woman told him as she stepped into the kitchen, only to turn around and go to the back porch. Her breath was gusting, and she was wringing her hands. "I've looked through the whole house, every inch of it, and they're gone." Etta Jean's voice cracked on that last word, and she began to sob.

Judson hated those tears, hated that the woman was an emotional wreck, but he couldn't take the time to soothe her. That would have to wait for later.

"Where's Addie?" he demanded.

Etta Jean pressed her fingers to her trembling mouth and shook her head. "I'm not sure. She thought she saw some tracks in the backyard, and she started following them out into the pasture. She told me to wait here until you showed up. We have to find them," she tacked on.

Yeah, they did, and that was Judson's main concern, but

at the moment, so was Addie. If someone had taken the babies, he didn't want her going after a kidnapper alone.

"Call the police station," Judson instructed, already heading out the back door. "Have the sheriff send out more deputies and do an Amber Alert on the twins."

That alert might have to be canceled within minutes if he found Addie and the babies right away, but in case that didn't happen, putting out the word on the missing babies would get a lot of resources in motion to try to locate them.

He didn't bother taking the steps. Judson jumped off the side of the porch and hurried through the yard, jogging and looking at the ground for any of those tracks that Addie had mentioned to Etta Jean. And he soon saw them.

Footprints in some mud.

It had rained just a couple of hours earlier, a good soaker that'd left the ground a soggy mess and had put a damp chill in the mid-October air. Not cold, exactly, but it sure as heck wasn't ideal conditions for babies to be out in this unless they were wrapped in blankets.

Would a kidnapper have done that?

Judson had to push that concern aside and just focus on finding Addie. Then he'd know what they were dealing with.

Well, hopefully he would.

Sometimes birth parents came after their kids who had been removed from their care. But that didn't apply in this case. The parents were dead, killed in a car accident shortly after the mother had been released from the hospital and the twins were still in a neonatal unit. The parents had been making a quick trip home to get a change of clothes and had ended up dying in a head-on collision caused by a drunk driver.

Lily and Rose had ended up here at the Horseshoe Ranch

with Addie just two weeks ago while the courts were sorting out next-of-kin issues. But maybe the next of kin, whoever that was, had decided to take matters into their own hands and snatch the girls. The odds were higher for that than abductions orchestrated by a stranger.

"Addie?" he shouted once he made it to the barn.

Again, there was no answer, but he saw more of those tracks in the mud. Not one set but two. Hell. Addie was following the kidnapper.

Judson picked up the pace, running now while keeping an eye out for more tracks and listening for, well, any damn thing.

Every bit of this pasture and the thick woods beyond it were familiar ground to him. Addie and he had spent a good chunk of their childhoods here, since she'd been in foster care as well. Those days, Mellie and Frank Carsten had run the place and had run it well, but after they'd died, Addie had stepped up to continue their legacy. And Judson knew Addie would do anything to protect the kids in her care.

Anything.

That's why he had to get to her.

Because she would absolutely confront a kidnapper if it meant getting the babies back. A confrontation that could get her hurt or killed.

He kept moving, even faster now. Kept following the tracks that led into the woods. There were old ranch trails threading through the trees and thick underbrush, and Judson headed toward the trail that was closest to the pasture. Again, he knew it well since it had become a favorite makeout spot for Addie and him when they were teenagers.

"Addie?" he tried again after he reached the trail.

This time, he got a response.

"Here," a voice said.

Relief flooded through him, robbing him of some breath, but it also got him moving in the direction of her voice. She was alive. That answered a whole bunch of his prayers, but Judson figured this ordeal wasn't over.

And it wasn't.

He soon saw that when he bolted through a cluster of trees and spotted Addie. She was standing on the trail, her gaze volleying in each direction. She stopped glancing around long enough for her gaze to land on him.

Judson saw the tears in her eyes, some on her cheeks, too, and there was a sense of sickening dread coming off her.

"I have to find them," she muttered, her voice a tangle of nerves and raw fear.

"We will," he said, though at the moment Judson had no idea how they were going to do that.

Addie looked so distraught. So broken. He wanted to pull her into his arms, to try to comfort her, but the best comfort he could give her was to figure out what had happened to the babies.

"Give me any details you have," he insisted, moving up the trail so he could look for more tracks. He saw some footprints but no signs that a vehicle had recently been here.

Addie moved, too, heading off the trail, her attention pinned to the ground. "I was, uh, getting the mail. Etta Jean was in the laundry room with the monitor while the twins were sleeping," she started but then stopped. "God, Judson. Rowena's out of jail."

That got his attention, not in a good way, either, and he whirled back around to face Addie. He didn't have to ask who she meant—Rowena Matthews was Addie's mother.

Except she wasn't.

When Addie was six, the truth had come out: that Rowena had stolen Addie when she'd been only a few weeks old. And Rowena had killed Addie's bio mom during the abduction.

"How the hell is Rowena out of jail when she's serving a life sentence?" Judson asked. "Did she escape?"

Addie shook her head. "No. She was released. I don't know the details, but someone from the parole board sent me a text. I got that about a half hour before I realized the twins were missing."

Damn it. That was tight timing. Of course, Rowena could have gotten out days ago and managed to set all of this up. Still, the woman had been in prison for twenty-eight years, and Judson would have thought her first move wouldn't have been to abduct another child.

But it was something he had to consider.

His phone dinged with a text, and he saw his boss's name on the screen. Sheriff Grace Granger. "The Amber Alert has been issued," he relayed to Addie after reading the message. "And Grace and the other deputies are on their way."

That didn't put any relief in Addie's eyes, probably because she understood it was going to take time to get a proper search organized. Time when the kidnapper could be whisking the babies away so they would never be found. That's why Addie and he needed to keep on looking, because every second counted.

While he kept moving, he also listened for any unusual sounds, along with firing off a text to Grace. *Rowena Matthews is out of jail. We need an APB on her.*

Grace might not immediately recognize the woman's name the way Judson had, but it wouldn't take his boss long to figure it out. And Grace wouldn't have any trouble getting an all-points bulletin or maybe even an arrest warrant for someone with Rowena's criminal history.

"You go that way," Addie said, pointing to the left. "And I'll go there." She then pointed to the right.

Judson definitely didn't like that plan. If it was Rowena who had done this, she had killed before and might kill again. Besides, the trail on the right led to the road, which was about a half mile away, and that was their best bet. The kidnapper could have left a vehicle there.

"We go together toward the road," he insisted, and to save Addie from arguing with him, he took off running in that direction.

Thankfully, Addie followed, staying right behind him. He definitely didn't want her out of his sight if they were dealing with Rowena. Or any other kidnapper, for that matter. Someone willing to sneak into a foster home and steal kids was probably desperate enough to kill anyone who got in their way.

This part of the trail was just that—a trail—no more than a foot wide in some places, and it was littered with fallen leaves, twigs and rocks. Unfortunately, there was no mud here to showcase footprints, but Judson thought he saw some spots where someone could have stepped.

"Other than Rowena, who might have done this?" Judson asked. "Have you had any run-ins with anyone?"

It wasn't an out-there question. Sometimes birth parents and family members threatened foster caregivers and social workers.

"No," she insisted as they kept moving.

"What about the twins' next of kin?" Judson pressed. "Any threats from any of them?"

"No," Addie repeated. "Just the opposite. Child Protective Services has located a couple of distant relatives, but none of them is interested in taking the girls. They're basically wards of the court for now."

So, an abduction likely wasn't linked to anything to do with the next of kin. But that left other possibilities. Bad ones. And Judson had to push those aside, too. He refused to even consider that the babies had been harmed.

He stopped when he reached a mudhole, and Judson spotted footprints—headed straight toward the road. That confirmed that Addie and he were heading in the right direction.

Judson paused to send Grace another text so she could get some deputies to that particular part of the road, but he stopped when he heard something. At first, he thought it could be some small animal, so he lifted his head and kept listening.

He heard it again.

And this time he was certain of something. That it wasn't an animal. It was a baby, and it was crying.

Addie's gaze sliced to his for just a split second. There was both shock and some relief in her eyes that Judson was sure was mirrored in his.

Without a word, they both took off running in the direction of the baby's cries, but they'd barely made it a few steps when Judson heard something else. Something that had his stomach twisting.

A car engine.

And it was speeding away.

Chapter Two

Addie ran as if Lily's and Rose's lives depended on it. Because they did. The babies could be in danger. Their kidnapper could be fleeing the scene and taking them heaven knew where.

Judson was flat-out running, too, and he raced past her, his arms pumping and his legs moving much faster than hers were capable of doing. Both of them had clearly gotten heavy slams of adrenaline. Both knew what was at stake.

If they didn't reach the babies in time, they might never see them again.

They might never know who had them or what was happening to them.

The possibility of that ate away at her like acid, and Addie wanted to scream. She didn't want any child to be put through what had been done to her—abducted and kept hidden away for six years by a woman who had claimed Addie as her own child before the truth had come to light.

No. Addie didn't want that for these precious babies. And she had to make sure history didn't repeat itself.

Just ahead, she saw the country road that led to both the town of Renegade Canyon and the interstate, depending on which direction you went. What Addie didn't see was the blasted car. Where the heck was it? Were they too late? Had the driver already managed to get away?

Still on the move, Judson ran to the end of the trail, coming to a skidding stop right at the edge of the road. His gaze whipped in both directions, and he must have seen someone or something, because he shouted.

"Stop!"

He continued to yell that one-word order, taking out his phone and clicking a photo before he started running again. This time on the road and to the left.

The direction of the interstate.

Addie got to him as fast as she could, and she soon saw what he was chasing. A black car. It was indeed speeding away, and in a blink, it disappeared around a steep curve.

"No," Addie shouted, and she started running again.

She was nowhere near close to catching up with the black car or Judson when she heard the sound of a vehicle behind her. For a moment, Addie thought it was the black car, that a miracle had happened and it had turned around so the driver could bring back those precious baby girls.

But it was a Renegade Canyon cruiser.

Addie instantly recognized the driver—Deputy Livvy Walsh, her foster sister—and she saw that Livvy's face was tight with nerves.

"Where's Judson running?" Livvy asked, lowering her window.

"After a black car," Addie blurted. "The babies are in there."

At least she hoped they were and that the black car wasn't some kind of decoy to get them searching in the wrong direction. But that was possible. Anything was at this point, and it occurred to her that the kidnapper could still be somewhere on that trail, hiding and waiting for a chance to escape.

"Get in," Livvy insisted. She reached over to open the passenger's door, and Addie practically dived inside.

Livvy took off, slamming her foot on the accelerator, which caused the tires to squeal against the asphalt. Judson no doubt heard it, because he spun toward them, already drawing his weapon, ready to respond to a possible threat. He quickly reholstered his gun, though, when he saw this wasn't a threat but rather help in the form of his fellow deputy.

Judson hurried toward them, and Livvy slowed so that he could jump into the back seat. The moment he was in, Livvy gunned the engine again and took off.

"Did you see the driver?" Livvy asked.

"No," Addie and Judson said in unison.

It was Judson who continued. "But I got a picture of the license plate. I'll call it in now."

Good. Addie wanted every cop in the area looking for this monster who'd taken Lily and Rose.

"I thought I saw someone in the back seat of the black car," Judson muttered. "But maybe not. It could have been a shadow or even the seat headrest."

Maybe the picture he'd taken would show that, but when Addie glanced back, she saw that Judson had only captured the license plate and part of the car's trunk.

The cruiser's tires squealed again when Livvy took the curve way too fast, and she had to fight to keep the cruiser on the asphalt. Because of the winding rural road, she immediately had to negotiate another curve, then another before they finally reached a straight stretch.

And Addie's heart dropped.

Because she couldn't see the black car. She couldn't

see any vehicle. It was possible that the driver was going so fast that they'd already managed to get out of sight, but there was also a chance that they'd pulled off onto a side road or a ranch trail.

"Keep watch," Livvy ordered them. "See if you spot it. I'm going to keep driving."

Addie did keep watch, but the scenery was practically flying by, and some of the trails were canopied with thick trees. If the driver had gone far enough down the trail, it could be impossible to see them from the road.

"The kidnapper and babies could still be on the southeast ranch trail," Addie managed to say. The muscles in her throat were so tight, it was hard for her to speak. "That's where Judson and I were when we heard one of the babies crying and the car engine."

Livvy nodded and used a voice command on her phone to contact dispatch. "I need someone to check the trail on the southeast side of the Horseshoe Ranch. That's the last known location of the missing infants."

"Will do," the dispatcher assured her and ended the call.

"The car is registered to an Yvette O'Dell," Judson relayed to them in between the conversation that he was having with someone at the sheriff's office.

Addie continued looking for the vehicle, but she also repeated the name several times to see if it was familiar. "That doesn't ring any bells. Who is she? And why would she take the babies?"

"Not sure yet," Judson replied.

Addie heard the hesitation in his voice and glanced back at him. "What?" she demanded.

There was some fresh worry in his already intense dark brown eyes. "Yvette has a record for being drunk and disorderly, and she got three DUIs before she lost her license. And her kids. Twins."

"Oh, God," Addie managed to say.

"No, the kids, her son and daughter, are alive," Judson was quick to add, cutting through what would have been some horrible worst-case scenarios for Addie. "They're in their early twenties now and were adopted by what appears to be a stable family, but Yvette lost custody of them when they were infants." He paused again. "For a while, her kids were fostered at the Horseshoe Ranch."

Addie groaned and fought back both fresh tears and a hot fury over this happening. Two decades ago, both Judson and she had been at the ranch in foster care, and kids came and went all the time. Sometimes they would be there for only a couple of days before their adoptive parents or other family members came to get them.

The Horseshoe hadn't changed much in those decades, so Yvette would likely have known not only the location of the ranch but where in the house to find the nursery. Added to that, the news and social media had been jammed with reports and comments about the orphaned Alcott twins. Yvette would have had all the info she needed to pull off this abduction.

But why?

Was she trying to replace her own kids? If so, why wait all this time? Or did Yvette have a personal connection to Lily and Rose?

Addie desperately wanted the answers to those questions, but for now, she focused on keeping watch, looking for that black car. Livvy continued to drive, slowing when they reached a four-way intersection. Then stopping. Livvy cursed and smacked her palm on the steering wheel. Addie totally understood her frustration.

Four roads and not another vehicle in sight.

A hoarse sob tore from Addie's mouth. This was crushing her heart, but she had to keep focusing. Had to keep thinking.

"Do you have a phone number for Yvette?" Addie asked.

"Getting it now," Judson replied.

Addie wanted to talk to her, wanted to try to convince the woman to surrender both herself and the babies. They were still so little, preemies, and they needed special formula every three to four hours. Addie thought if she could just speak to Yvette, she could make her understand the harm she might be doing.

"Got the number," Judson said, "and I'm calling it now."

From the back seat, Addie heard Judson's phone that was now on speaker. Heard the ringing on the other end of the line. The sound of each ring echoed through the cruiser. But there was no answer, and the call went to a generic voicemail, saying to leave a message.

Addie saw the debate Judson was having with himself. If he left a threatening message, Yvette might panic and do something even more horrible than she'd already done. Instead, Judson hung up and rang the police station again to request the contact info for both of Yvette's kids.

"It might not even be Yvette in the car," Livvy said, taking one of the concerns right out of Addie's mouth.

Yes, someone could have borrowed or stolen the vehicle, and if it was the latter, then that was only going to complicate the search. Addie didn't want more complications. She wanted those babies safely back at the ranch.

"I'm going to drive toward the interstate," Livvy let them know. "I'll have Grace contact the county sheriff's office so they can check these other routes."

Livvy took off again, using her hands-free function to

call Grace. Addie tuned that out and instead listened to the info Judson was getting. He apparently had the phone number for Yvette's daughter, Jennifer Rankin, and he tried to call her. Addie prayed Jennifer would answer.

And someone did.

"Hello," the woman barely managed to get out before Judson started talking.

"I'm Deputy Judson Docherty from Renegade Canyon PD," he said. "Is this Jennifer Rankin?"

"It is," she verified, and there was instant concern in her voice. "What's happened? What's wrong?"

"I'm looking for your bio mother, Yvette O'Dell. Do you have any idea where she is?" he asked.

"Yvette?" she questioned, and now there was some surprise mixed with the apprehension. "No, sorry, I don't know. I thought you were calling about my brother, Shane. I've been trying to reach him all morning, and he's not answering—" She stopped. "Wait, is he with Yvette?" And that concern skyrocketed. "Did Yvette do something to him?"

Addie's gaze snared Judson's. Their concerns were soaring even more as well.

"I'm not sure if your brother is with Yvette or not," Judson let Jennifer know. "I'm trying to locate her about another matter. When's the last time you saw her?"

"Last night," she said on a heavy sigh. "Before that, I hadn't seen or heard from her in weeks. But last night she just showed up at my apartment shortly after I got home from work. She was crying and going on about how sorry she was for what happened when Shane and I were kids. She does this about once a year, usually on our birthday. Today is our twenty-second birthday."

Oh God. Had that been some sort of trigger for Yvette to abduct the twins?

"What has Yvette done?" Jennifer asked, the dread coating her voice.

"We're not sure yet," Judson replied, obviously not spilling any details, "but it's imperative that I get in touch with her. If she contacts you, don't mention I'm looking for her. Just try to find out her location and then call me or the Renegade Canyon Sheriff's Office."

"Has Yvette done something bad?" Jennifer pressed. "Something to do with that foster ranch where Shane and I stayed before we were adopted?"

Everything inside Addie went still, and she waited for Judson's response. "Yvette's car was spotted near the Horseshoe Ranch," he finally said after a long pause. "Do you have any idea what she would have been doing there?"

Jennifer paused, too. "I'm not sure, but considering her state of mind last night, she might try to confront the woman who ran the place when Shane and I were living there."

Yvette couldn't have spoken to Jennifer's former foster mom, since Mellie was dead, but Addie was certain that Yvette, or anyone else for that matter, hadn't come to the door to ask about Mellie. They'd had no visitors all morning at the ranch.

Well, no visitor who'd rung the doorbell or paid a normal visit.

Obviously, someone had gotten in. Probably Yvette. And the fact that the car had been hidden on a trail meant the person hadn't had good intentions.

"Call me if you hear from Yvette," Judson repeated, and he ended the call with Jennifer. "I'm going to try to call Shane now," he let them know.

They didn't get lucky this time, because the call to Jennifer's twin brother went straight to voicemail, but Judson did leave a message asking the man to call him back immediately.

Livvy finished her call with Grace and continued the drive toward the interstate. With nothing else she could do, Addie kept looking for the black car. And tried not to give in to the panic that was building, building, building. She was fighting the tears again, too, when her phone rang.

The sound was so unexpected that she gasped, and because her hands were still trembling, it took her several moments to yank her phone from the pocket of her jeans. She didn't recognize the number on the phone, but she answered it right away on speaker, praying this was Yvette.

"Addie Jansen?" the caller—a woman—immediately asked.

"Yes," Addie verified, and she held her breath.

"I'm Courtney Mora, a social worker from San Antonio."

Addie's hopes vanished as quickly as they'd come. It wasn't unusual for her to get calls from social workers, and San Antonio was less than an hour from Renegade Canyon. Those calls were usually inquiries about possible placements for babies and kids that CPS had taken into custody.

"I'm sorry, but this isn't a good time," Addie muttered.

"I understand," Courtney replied. "I just saw the Amber Alert on the missing babies, and I might have some information."

Addie practically snapped to attention, and from the corner of her eye, she saw Judson have a similar reaction.

"What information?" Addie couldn't get out fast enough.

"Yvette O'Dell," the woman said, and just hearing the name gave Addie another slam of those raw nerves. "I was the social worker who removed her kids over two decades ago. Needless to say, I made an enemy of Yvette when I did that. She's tried her best to destroy me and my career."

This recap might be necessary, but Addie was anxious to get to the reason why Courtney had called. "Did Yvette come after the twins that I'm fostering now?" Addie demanded.

"Yes, I believe she did," Courtney replied. "Just yesterday, she showed up at my office to rant about how I ruined her life. I had security escort her out, but she had a wild look in her eyes, and I was worried she would try to do something reckless to get back at me. Perhaps she turned that recklessness on those babies."

Maybe, but again, motive wasn't as big a concern right now as finding Lily and Rose. "Do you have any idea where Yvette might have taken the twins?"

"I might. All those years ago when I took her children into custody, Yvette had them in an old fishing cabin. It used to belong to one of her father's friends. Anyway, if the cabin is still there, that's where she might have taken them."

"What's the address?" Addie pressed.

"I thought you'd ask for it so I looked it up before I called you. It's number three West Betterton Road, just outside of Bulverde."

From the back seat, Addie heard Judson phoning in the address so that someone could respond to the location. Since Bulverde wasn't that far away, only about ten miles, it was possible that Yvette could soon be there with the babies.

Livvy stopped, put the address in the GPS and started in that direction. They weren't far away, either, and would be there in under ten minutes. Sooner, Addie amended, considering the speed Livvy was driving.

"Thank you," Addie told Courtney.

"Glad I can help. I believe Yvette could be a very dangerous woman, and she needs to be stopped. I hope you can stop her. But be careful. There's no telling what she's capable of," she tacked on before ending the call.

Addie tried not to dwell on that *very dangerous* part and instead pinned her focus and attention on the road. Judging by the GPS, they'd be taking a lot of turns to get to the cabin.

Livvy slowed to take one of those turns, but then she slammed on the brakes. Clearly, she'd spotted the same thing Addie had: a red truck pulled just off the side of the road. There was a woman standing outside the vehicle, and she was waving to get their attention.

Addie's first thought was that the woman had broken down and needed help, but she looked more frantic than just a breakdown would warrant. Then again, she might have been out here for a while, and she might have seen the black car if it'd passed this way.

"Is that Yvette?" Livvy asked.

"No," Judson was quick to say. "Yvette's only forty-eight, and according to her latest DMV photo, she still has brown hair."

This person had to be in her late sixties, and her hair was pure gray. The moment Livvy stopped, the stranger hurried to the cruiser.

"She sped off before I could stop her," the woman said, her words rushing out with her racing breath.

"Who sped off?" Livvy asked. "And who are you? What's your name?"

"Nan Fredrick. My farm is just up the road a piece." She motioned behind her. "And as for the woman in the black car, I don't know who she was. Never saw her before in my life. I'd stopped to gather up some dried twigs to make a wreath, and she pulled up beside me. I was about to ask if something was wrong, but she got out and picked up two babies from her back seat."

Oh, mercy. The twins. They'd been here, right here.

"She shoved them into my arms and sped off," Nan went on. "I was about to call 911, but then I saw the cruiser and flagged you down."

Addie's breath had vanished, and she was glad Judson was able to voice what she wanted to know. "Where are the babies now?"

She pointed to the truck. "I laid them on the seat so I could use my phone. They were squirming, and I was afraid I'd drop them. I put my purse on the edge of the seat so they wouldn't fall off."

Before Nan had even finished her explanation, Addie heard a welcome sound. Actually, two sounds—fussing babies.

Addie bolted from the cruiser, sprinting toward the truck and throwing open the door the moment she reached it.

And there they were.

Lily and Rose were cuddled together in a pink blanket.

Chapter Three

Judson watched from the doorway of the den as Addie and Etta Jean each eased a sleeping baby into the pair of bassinets that had been set up in the room.

The change of location had been a necessity since the nursery itself was still being processed by the CSIs. Every inch of it would have to be checked for fibers or trace evidence to confirm that Yvette had indeed been in that room and had been the one who'd taken the babies.

Even after Addie and Etta Jean had the babies settled in, neither woman was eager to move away from the twins, and he figured it'd be a long time before Addie would want to let them out of her sight.

Especially since Yvette was still at large.

That's why some serious precautions had been taken, including posting a deputy with Nan Fredrick in case Yvette returned to try to get the twins from her. That probably wouldn't happen, since Yvette would likely assume that Nan had called the cops. Still, Yvette might be desperate enough to take the risk and return to the spot where she'd handed off Lily and Rose to the woman.

Another precaution was Judson had already decided that he'd be spending the rest of the day and the night at the Horseshoe Ranch. Because he, too, intended to keep an eye on Lily and Rose. Also on Addie and Etta Jean. It was just too risky to leave them alone, and despite Addie's now fairly calm demeanor, she was no doubt still going through an emotional upheaval.

Still, they'd gotten damn lucky. The twins had not only been found, but they'd also both gotten two thumbs-up from the pediatrician who'd examined them and said there wasn't a scratch or a mark on them. Getting that exam, and the clean bills of health, had required a trip to the hospital before Addie and he had finally been able to bring the girls back to the foster home shortly after noon.

As Judson had expected, Addie and Etta Jean continued to stay by the bassinets even though the babies were now sleeping after being fed, changed, burped and rocked to sleep. The last part of that hadn't taken long, since the girls had drifted right off despite having their routines, and their safety, shot to hell and back.

Judson had to tamp down his fury over what Yvette had done to them. Yes, the babies were safe and they hadn't been harmed, but any number of bad things could have happened, and Judson intended to make Yvette pay for what she had put them all through.

After several more minutes, Addie finally turned away from the bassinet, automatically reaching for the baby monitor that had been moved into the den along with other baby supplies. Then she shifted to look at Judson, their gazes connecting and holding.

Normally, when Addie and he had that kind of eye contact, he could see the heat there. The old chemistry between them. It'd been around for a long time, since they were teenagers, and more than once they'd given in to that lust and had kissed.

Later on, those kisses had escalated, and they'd landed

in bed a couple of times, but afterward, something had always pulled them apart. First, it'd been his stint in the military, and when he'd come home to sign on as a Renegade Canyon deputy, it'd been her brief engagement to another guy. After that particular relationship ended, the pulling apart had been instigated by them having to deal with Mellie's murder.

With Addie and him, it had always felt as if they were star-crossed, always something preventing them from even attempting something more than the occasional sex. That didn't stop the heat from coming, though. It was there, right now, but there was also something else. Judson could see the exhaustion and the worry etched all over Addie's face.

She went to him and walked straight into his arms. Definitely not something she usually did because of that attraction. But there was nothing normal about this day, about this moment.

Judson pulled her to him and hoped it helped. He hated seeing Addie eaten up like this.

"I know I need to give a statement to one of the deputies," she muttered. "But I don't want to go into the police station. I don't think Etta Jean does, either."

Both Etta Jean and Judson made a sound of agreement. "Grace said you could tell me the broad strokes of what happened," he let them both know, "but the official statement can wait until tomorrow now that the babies have been found."

Addie relaxed a little, but he still felt a lot of tension in her body.

"I'll stay in here with the babies if you two need to talk," Etta Jean offered. She seemed to relax some as well. "Then I can give you my statement. You can watch the twins on the monitor," she added to Addie.

Until Etta Jean said that last part, Addie seemed to be digging in her heels, ready to insist that she was staying put. But the conversation Judson and she needed to have would be emotional. Addie would likely cry, and he would almost certainly continue to get calls and texts about updates on the search for Yvette. All that chatter and noise could end up waking the babies before their naps were done.

"All right," Addie finally agreed.

Judson muttered a thanks to Etta Jean and eased back from Addie so he could take hold of her arm and lead her out of the den. Addie kept a firm grip on the monitor and pinned her attention to the screen as he took her up across the hall and into the living room.

"We don't have to talk in there," Addie said when she realized what direction they were going. "It's not a good place for you."

It wasn't. In fact, it held some hellish memories of where his unstable druggie mother had dumped him when he'd been just seven years old. Plenty old enough to catalog memories that no seven-year-old should have. Of the ugly names she'd called him. Of the rage that had twisted her face. That and the drugs had made her look like some kind of monster straight out of the fairy tales.

And she had indeed been a monster.

That'd been the reason Judson was removed from her custody, and her rage hadn't been because he was being placed in care but because she would no longer get the monthly payments from his late father's Social Security. Without the kid, she didn't have the money to feed her drug habit.

Thankfully, though, Frank and Mellie had quickly gotten the monster out of the house, so that had minimized the memories. Still, they were there, lurking around like ghosts, and it was the reason he usually avoided this room. Not today, though.

"The living room's close to the twins," he reminded her. And he would endure lots of ghosts, monsters and memories to give Addie the peace that'd come from only being steps away from the babies.

He had her sit on the sofa so he could take the spot right next to her. Judson also didn't want to be too far away from her when the tears started again.

And he didn't have to wait long for that.

They came right away, accompanied by a sob that tore from Addie's throat. He pulled her into his arms again and just let her cry it out.

"This is all my fault," she said in between the sobs. "I didn't lock the door, and I was distracted."

"Not your fault," he insisted right back. "An unlocked door isn't an invitation for Yvette to come in and take the twins."

It was true, but he doubted Addie would believe it. No. She would continue to blame herself when the blame sat solely with the woman who'd abducted Lily and Rose.

"When you can, tell me what was happening right before you realized the twins were missing," Judson said, keeping his voice calm despite the tornado of emotions whirling inside him. It was hell watching Addie go through this.

"I had just fed and put them down for a nap," she started after wiping away some of the tears. "It was my first time doing it solo. Usually, Etta Jean and I each take one. But I wanted to do it by myself just to make sure I could. That way, it'll free Etta Jean up to do other things, and with twins, there's a lot that needs to be done. Laundry, sterilizing bottles and such."

"And afterward?" he prompted when her voice cracked.

"What happened after you put the twins down for their nap?"

"Uh, after I made sure Lily and Rose were asleep, I took the monitor and stepped outside to get the mail. As I was coming back into the house, I got that text from the parole board to let me know Rowena was out of jail. I was upset," she added to that, and he knew that was a huge understatement. It had likely shaken her to the core. "I wanted to call the parole board, so I gave the monitor to Etta Jean to watch."

"And she was in the laundry room," Judson said.

Addie nodded. "I should have remembered to lock the front door, and I should have carried the monitor with me," she muttered on a groan.

"But you couldn't have watched the monitor and concentrated on the call you needed to make," Judson reminded her.

Again, Addie didn't seem to buy that, but she continued. "It took me a while to get through to someone, and I finally spoke to the head of the parole board, who told me that Rowena had been released for medical reasons. She apparently has cancer."

Prison officials sometimes did that, arranged an early release for an inmate with a terminal condition. But Judson would be looking deeper into Rowena's specific case. Rowena had been in jail for murdering Addie's mother, and even though that had been over three decades ago, it wasn't nearly enough time to serve for taking a life.

And putting Addie through hell and back.

As far as Judson was concerned, Rowena should have lived out her last days in prison. But the parole board obviously didn't agree. Judson knew that because he'd made some calls shortly after they'd gotten the babies back to the ranch, and he had been able to confirm that Rowena did indeed have pancreatic cancer, and her prognosis wasn't good. Supposedly, she had less than six months to live.

Judson had also been able to confirm something else: Rowena hadn't been anywhere near the ranch at the time the twins had been taken. She had been at a clinic in San Antonio, nearly an hour's drive away.

The sound of a car engine caused Judson's attention to shift to the windows, and he saw Livvy pull the cruiser to a stop in front of the house. He immediately got to his feet, hoping this was good news. Hoping that they'd found Yvette and had arrested the woman.

But then Judson saw that Livvy wasn't alone.

There was a tall, lanky, dark-haired man with her, and Judson recognized him from the photo that he'd pulled up when they'd been searching for the babies.

This was Shane, Yvette's son.

Good. Despite his sister's concern, Shane seemed unharmed, and he might be able to give them answers as to the whereabouts of his mother.

Judson went to the door to let them in, and he immediately looked at Livvy for an explanation for the visit.

"Shane, this is Deputy Judson Docherty," Livvy said. "And Addie Jansen," she added when Addie stepped up behind Judson. "After Shane heard about the APB on his mother, he came into the station."

"Pleased to meet you," Shane said, not actually looking at Addie and him but at the house. His gaze was sweeping over it, taking it all in. "Wish it were under different circumstances."

"Where's your mother?" Judson asked, well aware that he sounded abrupt. But the sooner they caught Yvette, the better, and he didn't want to waste time on small talk.

Shane sighed, shook his head and finally turned his gaze toward Addie and him. "I don't know where my mom is, but we need to find her." He opened his mouth, closed it and seemed to rethink what he'd been about to say. "We should probably sit down and talk."

Judson agreed, and he stepped back for him to enter, but Shane paused in the doorway, glancing around the foyer. "So, this is where CPS brought Jennifer and me when we were babies?"

"Yes," Addie murmured.

"I thought I might feel something. Some sense of recognition. But I don't." Shane shrugged. "I was just a baby, and I guess we didn't stay long. Just a couple of months before we were adopted."

That meshed with what Judson had read in the files that he'd managed to access while Lily and Rose were being examined at the hospital.

"You never came back here, just to have a look around?" Judson asked, and then he went with the question he actually wanted answered. "Maybe you came with Yvette?"

Something flashed through Shane's cool blue eyes. "No," he said. He didn't add anything else until they were in the living room, and then he turned to face them. "And I'm not sure my mother has been here recently, either."

Livvy didn't seem surprised by the comment, which meant Shane had likely already discussed this with her.

"I have a photograph of your mother's car fleeing the scene," Judson was quick to point out. "And the woman she left the babies with ID'd Yvette from a photo the cops showed her."

Shane nodded, slipped his hands into the pockets of his khakis. "My mother is a wonderful, loving, trusting woman," he said.

That didn't mesh with the info in the files. "She had a record, and she lost custody of you and your sister as kids," Judson argued.

"She did, but all her problems were caused by alcohol and drug abuse. Once she got sober, we reconnected, and I forgave her for what happened. And I love her," he tacked on to that.

That confession made Judson wonder if Shane was looking at this through rose-colored glasses. Maybe he wasn't able to see his mother's faults. Judson had gotten a totally different vibe about Yvette from Jennifer.

"You love her," Judson repeated. "Yet your sister was worried that Yvette had done something to you."

Shane rolled his eyes. "Jennifer always thinks the worst of our mother. Apparently, so do you, if you believe she stole those babies."

"If she didn't take them, then who did?" Judson demanded, wanting to hear this theory.

"Her husband, Trevor Cates," Shane supplied. He said both the title and the name as if they were the deadliest kind of venom.

"Husband?" Judson challenged. "There was nothing in Yvette's records about her being married."

"Because she married the son of a bitch just two weeks ago," Shane spat out. "Trevor, or Trev as she calls him, is a low-life gold digger who Mom met in rehab. My mother had just received a huge settlement that she got for being injured on the job, and I believe Trevor married her so he could get his hands on it. And I also think he might have taken the babies to try to set her up so that she'd be either arrested or killed."

Judson took a moment to process what Shane was saying, and looked at Livvy to get her take on it. "I ran a background check on Trevor," she said. "He's got a record for DUI and extortion, but there are no red flags to indicate he'd arrange a double kidnapping."

"He did it," Shane insisted. "I think Trevor coerced my mother into coming here. Maybe even used drugs or booze. He could have taken the babies and then fled with Mom and them."

"The witness didn't see anyone else in the car with your mother," Judson let him know.

Shane had a quick answer for that. "Trevor could have been hiding in the back seat. Or by then he could have had Mom drop him off somewhere."

Judson had to at least admit that those were possibilities. After all, he'd thought he had seen that shadow or something, but there was no proof that anyone else had been with Yvette.

"There has to be an easier way for Trevor to get his hands on your mother's money," Judson reminded Shane.

"Well, he can't outright kill her, because then he wouldn't be able to profit from his crime. I'm in law school," Shane added. "Trevor could also have triggered a relapse, something to send my mother over the edge, but he wouldn't necessarily get the money if she was back in rehab." He paused again, his forehead bunching up. "I think Trevor hoped the cops would kill her and then he'd be her beneficiary."

"Do you have any evidence whatsoever that would back up any of this?" Judson asked.

Shane sighed again and shook his head. "But I know in my gut that he's bad news and wants her dead. That's where I've been all morning, out looking for her. I wanted to find her and try to convince her to leave Trevor. I need you to talk to him. I need you to force him to tell us where my mom is and what he did to her."

"We'll contact him and see what he has to say," Judson assured him. "Do you have his address?" he added to Livvy.

She nodded. "It's just outside of Bulverde. Grace and two deputies are on the way there now. They should be there soon."

Good. Maybe they would find Yvette and could arrest her.

"My mother wouldn't have taken those babies without some kind of prodding," Shane insisted. "I'm sorry they were taken, sorry for the hell you must have gone through when they were missing, but my mom's not responsible."

The words had no sooner left his mouth than Judson's phone rang and he saw Deputy Eden Gallagher's name on the screen.

"Excuse me a second," Judson said, stepping out of the room to take the call. "Eden," he greeted when he was out of earshot. "Please tell me you found Yvette."

"Not Yvette, but there's a lot of blood," Eden replied. "And a big, bloody butcher knife. From what I can see, someone could have been seriously injured or even murdered here."

"But no body?" Judson pressed.

"No, no body, but the place isn't empty. There's someone here who might be able to give us answers." Eden paused. "Her daughter, Jennifer. FYI, Jennifer has blood on her hands, and she was holding the knife when we found her."

Chapter Four

Addie tried to focus just on taking care of the babies and not on the phone conversation that Judson had relayed to her a half hour earlier. But it was impossible for her to shove aside such important details.

Neither the Renegade Canyon PD nor the county sheriff's office had found Yvette's body. Or Yvette herself, if she was indeed alive. But they had found lots of blood at the woman's house. And since they had also found Yvette's daughter there as well, they were bringing her in for questioning.

Had Jennifer murdered her mother when she'd discovered that she'd abducted Lily and Rose? If so, then where was the body? Hopefully Jennifer would confess to that during interrogation, because as long as there was no concrete proof that Yvette was dead, the twins were still at risk. Yvette could return to the Horseshoe Ranch and try to take them again.

Of course, Addie wouldn't let that happen now that she was aware of the possible risk. Neither would Judson. He had stayed with her throughout this horrific ordeal, and he showed no signs of leaving.

Addie was beyond thankful for that. She wanted all the protection she could get for the babies. But as usual, whenever she was around Judson, part of her brain always shifted to the attraction between them. It was always there, a not-so-gentle tug in her body that just wouldn't go away. Well, not until her brain shifted to something else.

To their pasts.

Specifically, to conversations they'd had as teenagers.

They'd made a pact of sorts that they wouldn't have families of their own because of the brutality of their own nightmarish childhoods. Instead, they had agreed to focus on helping other troubled families and kids. It was the reason she became a foster parent and Judson had become a cop.

Addie didn't think either of them was anywhere near ready to ditch that pact and risk the fallout from those memories. Because, simply put, it was still too hard to deal with their pasts and keep up with the good things they hoped to accomplish in their lives.

The sound of footsteps yanked her out of her thoughts. Footsteps that she recognized before Judson even appeared in the doorway of her bedroom. Only fifteen minutes earlier, they'd moved the bassinets and some of the babies' things in here. With the CSIs still in the house, the cops coming and going, and the stream of phone calls and texts, Addie had wanted a quieter space for the twins. At six weeks old, Lily and Rose had endured enough upheavals and disruptions to last them a lifetime, and she wanted to eliminate more if possible.

Judson looked at the baby she was holding, then at the other infant, Lily, who was already asleep in the bassinet. Rose was asleep as well, and since both girls had already been fed and changed, they might nap for another hour or two. But Addie had wanted to hold the baby for a while longer. Correction: She needed to. And she would need to do the same with Lily after her next feeding.

For now, though, Addie could tell that Judson had something to tell her, so she eased Rose into her bassinet. She picked up the baby monitor even though she wasn't planning on going far. *Better safe than sorry* was her new motto. And she stepped into the hall with Judson.

"Did they find Yvette?" Addie whispered immediately.

He was equally quick in giving a response. Judson shook his head. "But there are still two teams out searching the area, and a sample of the blood has been taken to the lab. Both Yvette's and Trevor's DNA samples are on file, because they have criminal records."

"Trevor," she repeated on a heavy sigh.

Addie certainly hadn't forgotten about Yvette's husband, but she hadn't considered that the blood might be his. It could be, though, since after all, it was his house. The man wasn't responding to any attempts to contact him, so he was essentially missing. But did that mean Yvette or Jennifer had killed him? That was possible, but Addie was hoping the blood belonged to the woman who was the threat to the babies—Yvette.

"Has Jennifer made it to the police station yet, and has she said anything?" Addie asked.

Another shake of his head. "Eden texted that Jennifer seems to be in shock and just keeps muttering her mom's name. So Jennifer will need to be examined by a doctor before she can be questioned. They're at the hospital."

Addie groaned. She knew that couldn't be helped, that the cops had to follow the letter of the law on this, but an exam could delay Jennifer's interview. That meant a delay in getting the answers they needed.

Lily stirred a little, causing both of them to hurry back

into the room. But the baby didn't wake. After squirming around, she smiled and then settled.

"They're both beautiful babies," Judson muttered, "but they're even more beautiful when they smile."

Addie didn't tell him that it was probably a reaction to gas. Or that's what some experts thought, anyway. But she chose to believe it was the real deal and that it meant Lily was happy and content being home.

"Home," she heard herself whisper.

She hadn't intended to say that aloud, but it was a word she'd been giving a lot of thought to since the twins had arrived. So, Addie went with the rest of what had been on her mind before Yvette had come into the picture.

"I want to adopt them," she admitted.

Judson tore his gaze from the baby and looked at her. She saw the surprise in his eyes, which was the exact reaction she'd expected. She had worked at the Horseshoe Ranch for nearly a decade, and before that, Addie had been a social worker assisting couples who fostered. Not once during all those years had she considered adopting a baby.

Since she'd already given this plenty of thought, Addie figured that her quickly approaching thirty-fifth birthday was playing into her decision. She wasn't past the point of having her own biological children, but she also didn't want to wait much longer. But the biggest player in the decision was Mellie's murder. Life had suddenly felt way too short for Addie not to latch on to what she wanted.

"Uh, can you adopt them?" Judson asked.

"Legally, yes. No next of kin has stepped up to claim them, so eventually they'd be put up for adoption."

Of course, there would be plenty of people—couples—who would want them. And there might be a mark against her since the babies had been kidnapped while under her care. Addie prayed that wasn't the case, but she had to accept that it could play out that way.

"I'm not saying I want to adopt them because of nearly losing them," Addie went on. "I'd been giving it some thought since Lily and Rose were placed here." She paused. "You're thinking about that pact we made about never having our own families."

Judson shifted toward her, studying her, and made a sound of agreement. "I was also thinking you'd be a great mother."

That warmed her from head to toe. She hadn't realized how important it was for her to hear that from Judson. But it was.

"And that pact was made when we were hardly more than kids," Judson tacked on to that.

True, but it had made sense at the time. They had needed to focus on healing. On helping others. They still needed to do both of those things, but Addie felt she could do that while also being a mother to Lily and Rose.

"If you do adopt them, what will happen to the Horseshoe Ranch?" he added a moment later as he gently brushed his fingers over Lily's blond baby curls.

"I'll keep it going." That would mean hiring some extra help, but Addie was okay with that. "Mellie left me the ranch in her will, so legally it's mine, and this place is her legacy."

But there was one other important factor. The Horseshoe Ranch was her home, and it wouldn't feel like a real home without children around.

Addie's phone buzzed, and she stepped away from the bassinet and into the hall again. As she expected, Judson went with her, and both of them frowned when they saw Unknown Caller on her screen. Normally, calls like that were spam, but it occurred to her that this could be someone connected to the investigation.

She answered it, putting it on speaker, but she didn't even say any kind of greeting. She just waited to see what the caller would say.

"Addie?" the woman asked.

Even though it'd been a very long time since she had heard that voice, Addie instantly recognized it, and her heartbeat and her breathing thundered into overdrive. Because the voice belonged to the woman who'd kidnapped her and murdered her mother.

Rowena.

Oh, the memories came. Of course, they did. Impossible not to think of, or in this case hear, Rowena and not recall the horrible things she'd done. Some Addie had only read about. Others she had experienced firsthand.

Both before and after the abduction.

For a woman who had seemingly wanted a child badly enough to kill, Rowena hadn't known how to deal with motherhood. There had been lots of screaming at Addie. Cursing her. Belittling her.

And even more.

In those final months, Rowena had ended up pulling Addie from school and keeping her in a locked room. That had been the woman's downfall, because the school and neighbors had spoken up about not having seen Addie, and that in turn had launched an investigation, which, in turn, uncovered Rowena's crimes.

"How did you get my number?" Addie snapped.

Even though she felt plenty unnerved, she flat-out refused to let that show in her voice. Thankfully, she had enough anger as well, and she did let that come through.

Rowena sighed. "A friend got it for me."

"A friend," Addie repeated, and it came out in a snarl. "You mean someone you met in prison."

"Yes, please don't be mad at her," Rowena said. "I told her I needed to speak to you and try to make peace with you before… I, uh… I'm dying, Addie. I only have a few weeks to live."

"You can't make peace with me *ever*," Addie let her know and didn't give Rowena a chance to respond. She hit End Call and immediately blocked the number.

Now, she let out the emotions. The stormy mix of anger and the bitter memories. Suddenly, her legs felt way too shaky, and Judson must have noticed that, because he hooked his arm around her waist and pulled her to him.

She felt the instant relief go through her body. Felt his strength, too. And while this closeness might come back to haunt them, Addie gave in to it and sagged against him.

"I can get a no-contact restraining order," Judson murmured against her ear. "Or I can have the local cops go have a word with Rowena and tell her to back the hell off."

There was a firestorm of emotions in his voice, too, and again he was trying to protect her. That only fueled the closeness. Barriers that had always stood steady between them were coming down fast, and she wasn't going to try to stop it. Addie just stood there, taking every bit of the comfort he was giving her.

"It's okay," Addie let him know. "The blocked number should take care of her trying to contact me again."

She hoped so, anyway, and she made a mental note to find out if Rowena was well enough to attempt a visit to the Horseshoe. One thing was for certain: Addie wouldn't be emotionally blackmailed into seeing the woman.

"I don't need closure with Rowena," she spelled out to

Judson. "I shut her out of my life when I was six, and I'm not letting her back in."

"Good. Because I remember all those times she'd manage to call you or sneak a letter to you when you were a kid. It always ripped you apart."

It had, and Rowena had managed to do that three times before Mellie had made a trip to the prison and threatened the powers that be with legal action if they didn't stop the woman from contacting Addie in any way.

There had been no more letters or calls after that.

Until now, that is. And Addie refused to let even a sliver of Rowena climb back into her life.

Addie jolted when she heard the soft buzzing of a phone. Not hers this time, but Judson's, and it wasn't from an unknown caller but rather Livvy. Even though Addie was still feeling plenty shaky, she welcomed it, since this could be good news.

As Addie had done with her call from Rowena, Judson answered it, put it on speaker and alerted Livvy that she was listening in. However, he kept his attention pinned to Addie, no doubt checking to make sure she was okay.

She wasn't. Not yet.

But she was getting there. Every second that she spent being shaken up seemed like a victory for Rowena, and Addie didn't want to let the woman win.

"Just wanted to give you some updates," Livvy started the moment she was on the line. "Jennifer's being examined, and she seems to be coming out of the shock. She says she wants to give a statement. All we have to do now is wait for the okay from the doctor and we can take her to the station."

"Did she say if she killed her mother?" Judson asked, taking the question right out of Addie's mouth.

"No, and we advised her not to say anything about that, not until she was medically cleared," Livvy explained. "We didn't want a confession to be inadmissible if it turned out she wasn't declared competent to understand her rights."

Of course, that made sense, but it was still hard to wait. When Jennifer finally was able to be interviewed, maybe she would also spill about the location of Yvette's body.

"Will the two of you be coming into the station to observe Jennifer's interview?" Livvy asked.

Until Livvy mentioned that, Addie hadn't considered it. But she knew it was something she wanted to do. She wanted to hear firsthand what the woman had to say and maybe even speak to her afterward.

But Addie rethought that when she glanced at the babies. So did Judson, and she saw the concern on his face. She also figured he was champing at the bit to hear that interview.

"I don't want to risk leaving the twins," Addie muttered.

"Understood," Livvy was quick to say. "And I spoke to Grace about that. If Judson and you want to be here, Grace can send two deputies to the Horseshoe to do protective duty while you're away. Before you answer, I'll sweeten the offer by letting you know that you'll also likely be able to observe an interview with Shane."

"Shane?" Judson questioned. "Why are you bringing him back?"

"That's the next thing I need to tell you. I got a call about him," Livvy explained. "Remember when Shane said he'd never been to the Horseshoe as an adult? Well, that was a lie. Or a partial lie, anyway. He might not have actually gone there, but he was damn close. Holly Dennison was on her way into town and spotted a car turning on to the ranch road. A man in a small white car. Shane owns a white Ford Focus."

Addie knew Holly well since hers was the closest ranch to the Horseshoe. Holly was also observant, so Addie didn't doubt the validity of what the woman had seen. But why had Shane been here?

And better yet, why had he lied about it?

"Holly said she didn't think anything of it at the time," Livvy went on. "She thought it might be someone visiting a foster kid, but after the Amber Alert and APB were issued, the news media ran Yvette's pictures. One of them put up a photo of Yvette and her kids, and Holly recognized Shane as the man she saw taking the turn to the Horseshoe."

"When did she see him?" Judson pressed.

"Holly estimates that it was around nine this morning. That would have been before the twins were snatched. Yeah," Livvy muttered, no doubt anticipating the questions Judson and Addie had about that. "Trust me, I'll be asking Shane about that when he comes in for an interview. Not sure exactly when that'll be. He didn't answer when I tried to call him, but I left a voicemail and told him to come into the station right away."

Good. Because if Shane had played any part in the abduction, Addie wanted him to pay and pay hard for his actions.

"Hold a sec," Livvy said. "I have an incoming call from the lab."

Livvy put them on hold, giving Addie some time to think. Judson was obviously doing that, too, but neither one of them had much thinking time, because it was less than a minute before Livvy came back on the line.

"Well," Livvy said on a heavy sigh. "We've got a problem." And she continued after both Addie and Judson groaned. "The blood found in Trevor and Yvette's house doesn't belong to either of them."

"What?" Addie blurted. "Then whose is it?"

Livvy sighed again. "We're not sure. But according to the ME, there was enough to conclude that whoever's blood it is, that person is almost certainly dead. Now we need to find out who was probably murdered in that house."

Chapter Five

Judson watched as Addie gave each of the babies a kiss on the cheek, and while he figured she was trying to keep her nerves in check, he could tell she was worried about leaving them.

So was he.

With Yvette at large, Trevor missing and a possible unidentified dead body, there were a lot of moving parts in this investigation. But Judson was hoping that Jennifer and Shane would be able to fill in enough blanks for Renegade Canyon PD to figure out what the hell was going on.

"The twins will be safe," Judson heard Addie mutter, trying to reassure herself.

Judson couldn't promise Addie that nothing bad would happen—even if they stayed by the babies' sides. But he could promise that his fellow deputies Rory McClennan and Bennie Whitt would protect the girls with their lives. Added to that, Rory's brother, a wealthy rancher, had sent over two of his ranch hands, who would patrol the grounds.

Again, it wasn't foolproof, but everything was in place to make the situation as safe as possible.

"I won't leave this room even for a second while you're gone," Etta Jean promised Addie. She was standing by the bassinets, and she had a fierce, determined look on her face. "Go," the woman added. "Help them find Yvette so we can put all this behind us."

Judson hoped both things were possible. Finding Yvette was key, and then the healing could start. Still, it was going to be a long, long time before Addie would be able to stop looking over her shoulder for a possible threat.

He hated that. Hated that someone had shattered the peace and calm that Addie had worked so hard to find after Mellie's murder. She'd get that peace and calm back. And she'd find her new routine. But at the moment, it probably didn't feel like that.

Addie gave the girls yet another kiss, and she finally stepped away from the bassinets, turning toward him. Their gazes locked for a couple of moments. He didn't voice any reassurances or make any promises about the babies' safety. No need. Addie knew him through and through, and she was already aware that he had every possible precaution in place.

Including the cruiser parked out front.

Rory and Bennie had arrived in it just minutes earlier, and Addie and he would be using it to drive the short distance to the police station. The cruiser was bullet resistant, and even though Yvette hadn't fired any shots during the abduction, Judson had wanted the extra protection in place for Addie in case the woman came back for round two.

Judson's phone sounded with a text from Livvy, and he relayed the message to Addie. "Jennifer has just arrived at the station, and Shane is on his way."

Addie nodded, giving the babies one last look before she went to Judson. She added a thanks to both Rory and Bennie, who were already standing by to take up protection duty. Since both deputies had kids of their own and were experienced lawmen, Judson was hoping there wouldn't be any problems.

He didn't give Addie or Etta Jean an estimated time for their return. Too many unknowns there. It would depend on what Jennifer and Shane had to say in their respective interviews.

Or didn't say.

But if either of them were trying to hold on to their secrets, then maybe Grace and Livvy would get them to confess.

When they reached the front door, Judson used the keypad to unlock the cruiser, and moving fast, he got Addie outside and into the front seat. Best not to be in the open or on the roads any longer than necessary, so he pushed past the speed limit when they reached the highway.

Addie's phone rang, and he heard her sharp intake of breath. Probably because she thought it might be Rowena, but her shoulders relaxed when she saw the caller's ID. What she didn't do was take the call. She let it go to voicemail.

"It's my attorney who's handling the adoption," she let him know. "I'll need to talk to her, but not now. I'll call her back once the interviews are over and I'm home."

That made sense to him. Hard to focus on a phone conversation when watching to make sure someone wasn't about to shoot you.

"I didn't realize you'd already gotten a lawyer," Judson commented.

She made a sound of agreement and looked at him. "Does that bother you, that I want to do this?"

"No," he couldn't say fast enough. "Like I told you earlier, you'll make a great mom."

"Do I hear a *but* in there?" she came out and asked.

"No." Again, he said it fast. "You've got a lot on your plate right now, and I'm guessing the twins are like the bright lights waiting for you at the end of this ordeal."

She smiled, and it was good to see. Too bad it didn't last, because as Judson pulled in front of the police station, the smile went south.

"Move fast," Judson reminded her.

As he'd done back at the ranch, he hurried her inside to the chaos that went along with such a high-profile case. There were three different phone conversations going on from deputies in the bullpen. Another was going on in the sheriff's office. And another still at the receptionist's desk. A printer was chugging out something and making plenty of noise while doing it.

Despite all the noise and activity, Judson had no problem tuning it out and tuning in to the conversation taking place between Livvy and Shane.

"I didn't go to that damn ranch," Shane spat out, and he must have been alerted to Judson and Addie's arrival, because he shifted in their direction and repeated what he'd just said. This time, though, he added some more profanity.

"Deputy Walsh here is accusing me of lying and God knows what else," Shane went on, clearly in rant mode. "She thinks I kidnapped those kids. Well, I didn't."

Livvy looked as if ready to roll her eyes, but instead she motioned for Shane to follow her toward the interview rooms. She added a nod for Judson and Addie to come as well.

The change of location didn't cause Shane to hush. He just continued with his anger-filled tirade. "I was looking for my mother. That's why I was near that place. I turned in to the road, and when I didn't see her car, I made a U-turn and went looking for her elsewhere."

"I've already Mirandized him," Livvy said over her shoulder to Addie and Judson. "So he knows he has a right to have a lawyer and the right to stay silent. He's definitely not staying silent and has said he'll call in an attorney if and when he damn well pleases."

Livvy sounded more than a little satisfied about that not staying silent part despite the tongue-lashing Shane was giving her. And Judson understood why: Chatty suspects often spilled a lot more than they planned.

But the question was—did Shane have something illegal to spill?

Earlier at the ranch, Shane had admitted he'd been out looking for his mother, so that could explain why he was in or near Renegade Canyon. Another explanation, though, could be that he'd been there to assist his mother in committing a felony. Or to try to clean up after the one she'd already committed.

With Judson and Addie right behind them, Livvy led Shane to the second interview room. The door to the first one was closed, and Judson was betting that's where they had Jennifer waiting. Shane didn't go into the room, though. He whirled around to face the three of them.

"Look, all this is nonsense and a complete waste of your time and mine," Shane went on.

Neither Judson nor Livvy asked any questions, since any answers the man might give right now could perhaps be challenged later by his lawyer. But if it was info that Shane volunteered, even after being Mirandized, then it could turn out to be something the cops could use to prosecute him.

Shane huffed and folded his arms over his chest. "I was in that area because Mom talks about it a lot. She went through hell when CPS took Jennifer and me away from her. She was always going on about the Horseshoe Ranch and how the woman there, the manager, wouldn't let her see us kids."

The manager, Mellie, would have needed permission from the courts for a visit like that to happen, so Mellie had just been following the law. Along with protecting the children.

"Mom's been talking even more about that ranch lately," Shane continued. "I'm not sure why." He stopped, and some of the anger seemed to fade from his face. Either that or he was putting on an act. "Mom hasn't been herself since she hooked up with Trevor," he said in a barely audible mumble. "And I just didn't want her to do anything stupid, something she'd regret."

Judson didn't spell out that the evidence did point to Yvette kidnapping the twins. That wasn't in question since the farmer Nan Fredrick had seen Yvette with Lily and Rose. The big question now was had Yvette had an accomplice, and was that accomplice the man standing in front of them right now?

Shane seemed to stay in deep thought for several moments, and then he huffed as if frustrated that they weren't responding. "I'll call my lawyer after all," he snapped, going into the room and shutting the door behind him.

"You believe what he just said?" Addie asked, volleying glances at both Livvy and him.

Judson had to shrug. "It's possible that Yvette did talk about the Horseshoe, but why would Shane search that area? Why not go to his adoptive parents' house? Or his sister's? I'm sure Yvette talked about them, too."

"I'm hoping I'll find that out once his attorney shows," Livvy said, and then she motioned toward interview room one. "Jennifer hasn't lawyered up, so we'll be able to start with her…now," she amended when they heard the sound of footsteps and saw Grace making her way to them.

One look at his boss's face, though, and Judson knew she wasn't solely here for the interviews, that she had some news for them. And that the news wasn't good.

Grace launched right into that news. "I just got off the phone with the lab guys, and they ID'd the blood found in Trevor Cateses' house. It belongs to a social worker, Courtney Mora."

Addie gasped, and with her eyes wide, she snapped toward Judson. She obviously remembered that was the woman who'd called them earlier when they were searching for Yvette and the twins.

"She's the person who told us that Yvette was probably the one who'd taken the babies," Addie said.

Grace nodded. "Yes, I read that in Judson's preliminary report. I'm getting her phone records, but can you tell me where Miss Mora was when she made that call to you?"

Judson mentally went back through the conversation and had to shake his head. "She didn't say, and she sure as hell didn't mention she was on her way to the Cateses' house."

"She didn't say anything about that to anyone in her office, either," Grace replied. "In fact, she didn't show up for work today, and her boss was getting concerned. It was definitely out of the norm for her."

Hell. She must have taken it on herself to go to the house, looking for Yvette, and then…what? Yvette had killed her and left the knife behind for Jennifer to find and pick up?

Maybe.

Courtney had mentioned that Yvette hated her and had tried to ruin her life because she had been the social worker who'd removed Yvette's kids and placed them in foster care. So, maybe Yvette had returned from her canceled kidnapping plot to find a woman she hated in her home. But if that's what had happened, then where the heck was the body?

And where were Yvette and Trevor?

"What about Courtney's vehicle?" Addie asked. "Was it at the Cateses' house?"

"No," Grace answered. "There were no vehicles in the garage, and the one in front of the house belongs to Jennifer."

Then, that was another question that needed to be answered. It was possible someone had dropped Courtney off, or, heck, maybe she had even managed to get an Uber or a taxi to take her that far. But if she'd taken those particular forms of transportation, there should be a record of it.

"Along with finding the blood and Jennifer at the Cateses' house," Grace went on several seconds later, "the CSIs also found some drugs. Rohypnol and Valium."

"That's a strange combination." Judson shook his head. "The date rape drug and anxiety meds. Any idea who was taking them? Or who was giving them to someone else?"

"Don't have a clue yet, but they were in the nightstand drawer of the main bedroom, so the CSIs might be able to determine through prints who used that drawer the most. Or whose prints are on the actual plastic bags that contained them." Grace checked her watch. "It's going to take an hour or two to get those phone records or any other info from the CSIs and ME. Let's get moving with interviewing Jennifer so you two can get back to the Horseshoe. How are the twins doing, by the way?"

"They're fine," Addie assured her. "They don't seem to be experiencing any kind of trauma."

They weren't, and Judson hoped it stayed that way. He had no idea what babies that young could experience, but he hoped they never sensed or remembered any part of that ordeal.

"The Bulverde cops are on the way to Miss Mora's next of kin to tell them about the blood that was found," Grace went on. "So, I don't want to specifically mention the social worker by name until I'm certain her family knows. But I do intend to bring her up in a roundabout way to Jennifer, just to see what she has to say." She paused. "Because it's possible Jennifer killed her, and I want to know why."

It was indeed possible, since Jennifer had been found at the scene with a knife and blood on her hands. And Jennifer might have had motive to commit that murder if she also blamed Courtney for Shane and her being taken from Yvette's custody. The one problem with the theory was that during their earlier phone conversation with Jennifer, the only animosity she'd shown was toward Yvette. So why would she be so upset about being removed from her home all those years ago?

"Does Jennifer know her brother is here?" Judson asked.

Grace shook her head. "I don't want the two of them speaking until after their interviews. She has asked for him," Grace added. "For her boyfriend, too."

"Elijah Banks," Livvy provided. "He's a personal trainer at a gym in San Antonio, and an amateur boxer. We're trying to get in touch with him now."

Good. Maybe the boyfriend would be able to give them some insight into all of this.

"If Jennifer says something you want me to press her on, just send me a text. I'll see what I can do," Grace told Addie and him, and then she and Livvy went into the interview room.

Judson led Addie to the small area next to interview. It wasn't much bigger than a closet, but it had some chairs and a small table with a laptop. The screen was blank at first, but when Grace engaged recording, the feed from the interview popped up. Judson could see Jennifer pacing. And seemingly ready to jump out of her skin.

"I didn't kill anyone," Jennifer immediately blurted.

Grace motioned for the woman to sit, and Livvy and she took the seats across from her. Judson and Addie sat as well. Side by side. Or rather hip by hip, since that was all the space they had.

"I didn't kill anyone," Jennifer repeated, but again Grace motioned for her to hold off while she recited the case number, time, date and those present.

"Jennifer, Deputy Walsh has already read your Miranda rights, but could you state for the record if you understand them or if you want them repeated?" Grace instructed.

"I understand them and don't need to hear them again." Once more, Jennifer's words were rushed, running together and filled with her heavy breaths. "I just want you to put down in your record that I didn't kill anyone. I was framed."

Grace eased back in her chair. "I'm listening."

Jennifer nodded and seemed to mentally throttle back a little. "I, uh…" she began but then stopped. "I guess I should start with the phone call I got from one of your deputies. Docherty, I think, was his name. He asked where my mother was. I didn't know," she insisted. "But as soon as I got off the phone with him, I started driving out to her house. Or rather, *Trevor's* house."

Judson noted that like Shane, there was some venom in Jennifer's voice when she mentioned the man's name. It made him want to dig harder and deeper to find this Trevor. Then again, he could say the same for Yvette. It was possible the two had fled together and were in hiding.

"Since no one knew where Shane was," Jennifer went on, "I was worried that Yvette had done something to him."

"Like what?" Grace pressed when Jennifer fell silent.

Jennifer sighed and pushed some strands of long blond hair from her face. "I don't know." But it didn't take her but a couple of seconds to amend that. "All right, I thought she'd convinced him to do something that could get him hurt. Shane can be...gullible sometimes. I thought maybe Yvette had talked him into helping her take those babies." She paused again, looked at Grace. "Is that what happened? Did Shane help her?"

As Judson expected, Grace didn't respond to that question. Nor did she mention anything about Shane being seen in the area around the time of the abductions. Instead, Grace flipped through her notes as if checking some kind of details.

"So, you went to the house looking for Shane and Yvette. What happened then?" Grace pressed.

"Not especially looking for Yvette," Jennifer corrected. "But my brother, yes. When I got there, there were no cars in the driveway, and that's where Shane would have parked had he been there. Still, I wanted to check for myself, so I went to knock on the front door. That's when I saw the door was slightly ajar. I eased it open a little more and called out for Shane."

Jennifer stopped, and she pressed her fingers to her mouth. Probably to stop the sob that made it past her lips anyway.

"I saw some blood on the floor," the woman continued. Both she and her voice were now shaking. "Blood on the walls, too. God, it was everywhere," she added on another sob. "I thought it was Shane's, that Yvette had done something to him, so I ran through the house, screaming out his name. No one answered. No one was there. Just all that blood."

"How did the knife get in your hands?" Grace asked.

"I, uh, picked it up," Jennifer admitted. "I thought maybe if it was Shane's blood, then Yvette, or if not her, someone else could be hiding in the house. I wanted to look for them. Wanted to look for Shane. And that's what I was doing when you and the deputies showed up."

Judson was nowhere near convinced Jennifer was telling the truth. But it was possible Jennifer had killed Courtney because she'd mistaken her for Yvette. Though that felt like a huge stretch. After all, it was broad daylight, so both women would be easy to recognize. Still, it could have happened that way.

Maybe.

But if Jennifer was a killer, then why hadn't she disposed of the knife at the same time she had the body?

"Is Yvette dead?" Jennifer came out and asked. "Was that her blood all over the house?"

"We're looking into that," Grace settled for saying. "Who do you think might have had the motive to do that?"

Jennifer laughed, a single burst of air, but there was no humor in it. "Yvette was a 'recovering' drug addict and alcoholic." She put *recovering* in air quotes. "I'm sure she's made a lot of enemies over the years."

"Including you?" Livvy asked.

"Including me," Jennifer verified. She paused for what seemed like a full minute. "And Shane."

"Shane?" Grace immediately questioned.

Both Judson and Addie moved closer to the monitor. Obviously, neither of them had expected Jennifer to admit that.

Jennifer dragged in a long breath before she said anything else. "Shane didn't want Yvette involved with Trevor.

He thought Trevor was only after Yvette's money. I agree with that, by the way. But Yvette couldn't seem to see that, and she refused to have him sign a prenup or try to protect her assets in any kind of way." Another pause. "She and Shane argued about that."

"Did you actually hear any of these arguments, or is this something Shane told you?" Grace asked.

"I heard two phone conversations he had with her. Shane made those calls when he was pleading with her to do the prenup or else sign over half of her estate to him so that he could keep the money safe from Trevor. We're talking nearly a half million dollars," she explained. "But Yvette flat-out refused, and Shane was furious."

"Furious enough to threaten her?" Livvy pressed.

Jennifer didn't jump to deny that, and she finally nodded. "Shane said some harsh things to her. Things she deserved."

Then Grace asked the question that was flashing through Judson's head. "Did he threaten to kill her?"

Jennifer groaned and shook her head, but the headshake didn't seem to be a denial. "Yes. But he didn't mean it," she was quick to add. "I know he didn't."

The woman didn't seem at all convinced of that last part. And neither was Judson. Money was always a powerful motive. But that was a motive for murdering Yvette, not Courtney. Unless…

"If Shane helped his mother set up the twins' abduction, maybe Courtney found out about that," Judson muttered.

Addie's immediate sound of agreement let him know she was thinking the same thing. "Shane and Yvette could have been talking about it, or arguing about it, when Courtney showed up. If she heard something they hadn't wanted her to hear, they might have killed her."

She stopped, her forehead bunching up, and made a sigh of frustration as something else seemed to occur to her.

"It could have played out a different way," Addie concluded. "If Courtney had indeed heard that Shane had had a part in taking the twins, then Jennifer might have wanted to silence her to protect her brother."

Yeah, Judson could see that happening, too. And that meant they were essentially back to square one in this investigation.

"I really need to see Shane now," Jennifer pleaded. "And Elijah. He'll be worried about me."

At the mention of the boyfriend, Judson was reminded they possibly had another key player in this case. One who wasn't responding to attempts to contact him. Was that because he had something to hide? Of course, it could also be that he didn't care enough about Jennifer to want to get caught up in this.

Grace's phone made a sound dinging sound, and when she glanced at the screen, she immediately got to her feet. "Interview paused," Grace said, heading toward the door.

"Sheriff Granger is exiting the room," Livvy added for the benefit of the recording.

Addie and Judson stood, too, and came out of observation just as Grace was stepping into the hall.

"The search team found Courtney in her car about a half mile from the Cateses'," Grace let them know. "She's alive."

"Alive," Addie said through a rush of breath.

"Barely," Grace qualified. "The EMTs are rushing her to the hospital now, and that's where I'm heading. I want her to tell me who left her for dead."

Chapter Six

Addie sat in Grace's office, as Grace had instructed, while Judson worked at her desk. The sheriff was driving to the Bulverde hospital to try to question Courtney.

The waiting was hard, but Judson was making good use of the time while going through reports and doing some paperwork. In fact, all the deputies were doing that, including a reserve cop who Grace had called in to assist with the extra workload.

She imagined that Grace was seriously shorthanded, what with multiple facets of an investigation going on. That's why Addie was thankful Grace had given Judson the time off to do personal protection detail. Addie hated to add to Grace's manpower burdens, but she hated more that the twins wouldn't have someone around who could protect them. The two deputies with them now were a good substitute, temporarily anyway, but Addie didn't trust anyone more than Judson when it came to keeping Lily and Rose safe.

At the thought of the girls, Addie checked her phone again and reread the last text she'd gotten from Etta Jean. It'd come just fifteen minutes earlier, and there'd been one a half hour before that. Addie was thankful for each and every one of the messages, but especially this one, since

Etta Jean had included a photo of the babies, sleeping peacefully in their bassinets.

"The CSIs are going over Courtney's car now," Judson relayed, obviously reading from a text update he'd just received. "Her clothes will be processed, too, once the EMTs are able to bag them. It's hard to stab someone and not leave at least a little of your own DNA behind."

Addie hoped that was the case here. Or better yet, she hoped that maybe Courtney herself would be able to give them that info. That was the reason Grace had decided to keep Jennifer in custody a while longer. There wasn't enough evidence to actually arrest her, but that could change in a blink if Courtney named Jennifer as her attacker.

"The CSIs also checked for prints on the two plastic bags of drugs," Judson went on. "There are some smudges and what appear to be paper fibers on the outsides, as if someone tried to wipe the bags clean. Still, the lab might be able to enhance them enough to get a match."

She considered that a moment. The drugs were yet another question mark in an investigation crammed with questions.

"How much access did Jennifer and Shane have to the Cateses' house?" Addie asked.

"Shane was there recently. Jennifer claimed she'd never been there before today." He paused. "You're thinking one of them could have planted the drugs."

She nodded. "Maybe to set Trevor up and make it look as if he was drugging Yvette. Or could they have done that to discredit him in Yvette's eyes?"

"Possibly. Both Jennifer and Shane have made it clear they despise their stepfather. There's no evidence, though, that Yvette was ever given or took the drugs. And by that, I mean no witness statements or tox reports."

That was true, and Addie would have given that more thought as well if the sound of approaching footsteps hadn't caught her attention. She was still on edge enough to get to her feet, ready to defend herself.

A moment later, Livvy stepped into the doorway, and she wasn't alone—Shane and his lawyer were right behind her. Addie recalled the lawyer introducing himself as Ira Covington when he'd arrived at the police station shortly after Grace had left for the hospital.

"Grace texted and said she's decided to reschedule Shane's interview," Livvy let them know.

"The cops have no grounds whatsoever to hold my client," the lawyer piped up, causing Livvy to roll her eyes. Obviously, she was tired of dealing with the attorney's complaints.

"The cops have rescheduled your client's interview for tomorrow morning at eight," Livvy replied, mimicking the same snappy tone as the lawyer's.

"I'd like to see my sister before I leave," Shane said, aiming that request at Judson.

"I've already told him no," Livvy volunteered.

"Then you won't be seeing her." Judson aimed that remark at Shane.

Shane huffed. "But if there's no cause to hold me, the same applies to her. You should have her come back in tomorrow, too. For now, I can take her home so she can get some rest."

"The same doesn't apply," Judson was quick to point out, but he didn't elaborate, holding on to the details of Jennifer being found with a knife in her hand. "And the reason you're not speaking to her is because we don't want her statement skewed by any outside information. It needs to be an accurate account from her perspective of what actually happened."

The lawyer stepped into the doorway, bumping Livvy as if trying to nudge her aside. But Livvy held her ground.

"Are you saying you believe my client and his sister will fabricate something if they have a simple conversation?" Covington demanded.

Judson gave him a hard stare. "Yes. I'm saying it's possible. And it might not even be intentional or with criminal intent," he added, cutting off what appeared to be the start of a rant from the lawyer. "It's best if Jennifer gives us a clear account of what happened at her mother's house. We don't want her to add or draw conclusions from anything that anyone else says. That includes her brother."

Clearly, neither Covington nor Shane cared much for that answer, but they must have sensed the deputies weren't going to change their minds. The lawyer muttered something about seeing them in the morning and motioned for his client to follow him out of the building.

Because Addie kept her attention on them, she saw the beefy man with sandy-brown hair approach Shane and Covington just outside the door. She couldn't tell what the three were saying, but it was obvious Shane knew this man.

Obvious, too, that the man was furious.

After a short conversation with Shane, the man practically threw open the door to the police station.

"Where the hell is Jennifer?" he snarled.

"That's Elijah Banks, Jennifer's boyfriend," Judson informed Addie. "I recognize him from his DMV photo."

Both Livvy and Judson turned to face the man. Addie moved as well, positioning herself right behind them and looking over their shoulders so she could see Elijah try to storm toward them.

Try but fail.

Deputy Garrison Zimmer blocked him and tipped his head to the metal detector. “Walk through there,” Garrison ordered.

Elijah looked ready to argue with that, too, but, muttering obscenities under his breath, he finally went through. And immediately set off the alarms. Garrison drew his gun, and while he didn’t actually aim it at Elijah, it caused the young man to thrust his hands in the air.

“There’s a sign on the door that reads, ‘No firearms or knives allowed on these premises except for law enforcement officers,’” Garrison pointed out. “There’s even a picture of a gun with a red line drawn through it.”

“I didn’t notice it, all right,” Elijah snapped. “All I was thinking about was getting in here to see my girlfriend.”

“Using just two fingers, remove your weapon and place it there,” Garrison instructed, motioning toward a box on the table next to the metal detector.

Elijah glared at him, but did as he was told and produced a small handgun from the back waist of his bulky cargo pants. He put the gun in the box and lowered his other hand.

While Garrison dealt with locking up the gun in the box, Judson walked through the bullpen to reach Elijah.

“We’ve been trying to reach you for hours,” Judson told the man. “Where were you?”

“At work,” Elijah said without hesitation. “And then training for a boxing match.” He tapped a bruise on his right cheekbone. “I don’t answer my phone or check my messages when I’m at the gym or in the ring. Good way to get your face busted. When I finished and listened to the voicemails, I drove straight here. Now, I want to see Jennifer."

"I'm sorry, but Jennifer can't have visitors," Judson informed him. "And Shane probably told you that when you saw him outside."

Elijah cursed. "Shane's a wimp. I figured he didn't press hard enough about that." He rammed his thumb against his chest. "But I will see her."

"You won't." Judson returned the fierce stare the man was giving him. "I can have her contact you after her interview."

Oh, Elijah didn't care for that, and the fury raced through his stormy gray eyes. "Is Jennifer under arrest?" he demanded to know.

"Not at the moment, but she's been detained for questioning," Judson replied.

"Why?" the man insisted. "What is it you think she did?"

"I'm not at liberty to discuss that with you" was Judson's reply.

Elijah cursed some more. "Did that train wreck Yvette have something to do with this? If so, you shouldn't believe a word she says. The woman is a walking, talking bag of… lies," he finally finished, but Addie thought he wanted to use much stronger language to describe her.

That clearly got Judson's attention. "You know Yvette?"

"Of course I know her. She's always trying to worm her way back into Jennifer's life. Always boo-hooing about *forgive me, baby*," he said in a mock-pitiful voice. "As if. That woman has put Jennifer through hell and back over the years."

"What about Trevor?" Judson pushed. "Has he done that, too?"

Elijah had a surprising response. His glare shifted to a

smirk. "Trevor's lazy and worthless, and he'll suck every penny out of Yvette. Personally, I hope he does. That'll be exactly what Yvette deserves."

So, maybe that meant Jennifer wasn't concerned about Trevor's possible gold-digging. Unlike Shane, who seemed to want his share of his mother's money.

"Any idea where Yvette and Trevor are?" Judson asked.

"Hell if I know. Last I checked, I wasn't their keeper." He paused again. "Did one of them do something to hurt Jennifer?"

Judson turned the question around on him. "What makes you ask that? Has one of them hurt her before?"

Elijah opened his mouth. Closed it. "I don't know. Let me speak to Jennifer's lawyer," he tacked on to that.

"She doesn't have one," Livvy provided.

"And you're hounding her anyway?" Elijah howled. He started shaking his head. "No, no, no," he strung out. "That's not gonna happen. No more questions until she has a lawyer."

"That's not your call," Judson said.

"We'll see about that," the man snapped, already taking out his phone. He turned and headed back toward Garrison and the metal detector. "I want my gun, and I'll be back when I get Jennifer the legal help she needs."

Once Elijah was on the other side of the metal detector, Garrison picked up the gun, but he didn't hand it back to Elijah until the man was outside the door. Then Garrison tapped the sign about no firearms.

Elijah gutted out a single word of raw profanity and walked away while he scrolled through his phone. No doubt to contact a lawyer. He apparently found what he was looking for, because he made a call as he got into his dark blue truck and drove away.

Judson cursed as well. "If a lawyer shows up, the interview probably won't happen today. There'll likely be lots of legal wrangling…well, unless Jennifer flat-out refuses to have legal counsel."

"She probably won't refuse if she knows Elijah arranged it," Livvy pointed out. She sighed and glanced at both Addie and Judson. "Why don't you two go back to the ranch? I figure you're anxious to be with the twins."

Addie was indeed anxious, so when Judson nodded, she was ready to go despite the hesitation Addie saw on his face. He no doubt felt swamped with the amount of info that needed to be processed.

"Send me some of the workload," Judson told Livvy. "I'll go through any and all reports and summarize them for the rest of the team."

"I can do that," Livvy said. "It'll free me up to try to find Trevor and Yvette. And to deal with Jennifer. I'm not sure how long she'll sit in interview without putting up an argument."

Yes, and coupled with a potential attorney, Addie could understand why the interview likely wouldn't happen anytime soon. It was possible a lawyer would demand a thorough psychological eval of his client rather than relying on the expertise of a small-town ER doctor. Especially a doctor who would know all the members of the police force.

"I'll get my purse," Addie said, heading back into Grace's office where she'd left it. However, she'd barely made it a step before Livvy's phone rang.

"It's Grace," Livvy muttered, and she immediately took the call, putting it on speaker. "I'm here with Addie and Judson, who are listening in. Garrison, too," she added when the other deputy joined them.

"I made it to the hospital in Bulverde," Grace started,

and Addie's stomach automatically clenched. Because she could tell from Grace's tone that this wasn't going to be good news. "Courtney died before the EMTs could even get her out of the ambulance."

Addie groaned. The three deputies each did some cursing. "Did Courtney manage to say anything to the EMTs?" Judson asked.

"No. She never even regained consciousness." Grace's heavy sigh came through loud and clear. "So, this is officially a murder investigation. *Ours*," she emphasized. "The area where Courtney was found is in the county sheriff office's jurisdiction, but since this is possibly connected to the twins' abduction, the county is handing it to us. I'm heading back to the station now to create a file on it. What's going on there?" she tacked on.

"We got a visit from Jennifer's boyfriend," Livvy let her boss know. "I can brief you on that since Addie and Judson were about to leave."

"Good," Grace said. "No need for them to be there, and they'll be better off at the ranch. Once you're back at the Horseshoe, just send Rory or Bennie back to the station. One of them can stay there for a while until...well, until things are more stabilized than they are right now."

"Thank you," Addie and Judson said together.

Addie took her purse, and she and Judson headed out while Livvy got started with the recap of Elijah's visit. Grace probably wasn't going to be any happier about it than the rest of them were.

They were only steps from the door when a landline phone rang, and seconds after Garrison answered it, the deputy called out, "I have Trevor Cates on the line."

That stopped them in their tracks, and they hurried back to the desk. "Put the call on speaker," Judson instructed the younger deputy, and Livvy moved closer, holding up her phone so that Grace could no doubt hear as well.

"This is Deputy Judson Docherty," he said.

"Trevor Cates," the man replied, and he sounded all frantic nerves. "I've been camping. There's no cell service out there, and I just saw all the missed calls. Some from Jennifer, others from Shane and three from Renegade Canyon PD. What the hell is going on?"

Addie figured Judson had plenty of questions, but he went with a simple one. "Where are you right now?" he asked.

"On the way back to my house. I pulled over when I finally got out of the dead spot and was able to check my phone," he explained. "When I saw your messages, I called right away."

"Don't go home," Judson insisted, and he dragged in a long breath. "A woman was attacked in your house, and there's a team of investigators inside and on the grounds."

"What?" Trevor blurted, his voice practically a shout now. "What do you mean? What woman was attacked? Was it Yvette?"

Again, Judson took his time answering. "Where is your wife, Mr. Cates?"

"Uh, I assumed she was at the house. At our home," he amended. "Isn't she? God, is she hurt?"

"We're not sure. We've been looking for your wife but haven't been able to contact her."

"Wait, hold on," Trevor insisted, and now there was some panic rising in his tone. Maybe the real deal. Maybe fake. Addie couldn't tell. "Just wait," he repeated. "I'm going to try calling Yvette now."

Judson didn't stop him from doing that. Trevor put them on hold, hopefully to make that call and not flee. Addie also hoped that once he came back on the line, he'd have answers about Yvette's location.

But that didn't happen.

"She's not answering," Trevor relayed several seconds later. The panic in his voice had gone up significantly. "Is my wife all right?"

"Like I said, we don't know. We need to speak to both of you," Judson informed him.

"Of course," Trevor muttered, and he repeated that several times. "But I want to look for her. I want to try to find her. I have to know if something happened to her." He stopped, groaned. "You said a woman was attacked in my house. Was it Yvette?" he demanded again.

"No," Judson replied, "it was someone else, but I can't discuss the details with you. Best if you come in and give that statement."

"Okay," Trevor said after a long pause. "But can it wait until morning? It'd be dark before I could get to Renegade Canyon, and I have trouble driving at night. Plus, I guess I need to find some place to stay since my home is a crime scene." His voice broke on those last two words.

Livvy and Judson exchanged a long look, probably trying to decide the timing for the interview since Shane would be coming back in at eight. Jennifer might possibly still be here as well.

"Have him come at 8:00 a.m.," Livvy mouthed.

Judson gave a quick nod, indicating he wanted the same thing. "Be here at eight tomorrow morning," he told Trevor. "And if you do hear from or find your wife, call us immediately."

"Will do," Trevor assured them, and he ended the call.

"It'll be interesting to see how Shane reacts to Trevor and vice versa," Livvy muttered.

"Yeah, and maybe by then, we'll know where Yvette is," Judson added, and they started for the door again. "I also want to verify some things about Trevor. The camping trip, for one thing. I want to make sure he was where he said he was. And that bit about him not being able to drive at night. He's only forty-nine, and that's not usually something that happens to someone in his age bracket."

Addie agreed, but she didn't ask the questions on her mind until after Judson and she were in the cruiser and driving toward the ranch. "I understand why Trevor might lie about the camping. He could be using that as a sort of alibi to make us believe he was nowhere near Yvette or Courtney today. But why would he lie about the driving to stall the interview?"

"Maybe he wants to find Yvette first." Judson stopped talking, scrubbed his hand over his face and groaned. "Or, hell, maybe he's telling the truth and has no part in any of this. It's hard to trust the guy based on what Yvette's kids have said about him, but none of what they spilled could have been the truth."

It was frustrating not knowing if Trevor was a killer, but maybe something incriminating would come out during the interview. If not incriminating about himself, then maybe for one of their other three suspects—Elijah, Shane or Jennifer.

Addie's phone sounded with a text, and she saw it was from Etta Jean. No actual message, just a photo of the twins side by side on a quilt on the floor, awake and alert. Etta Jean had even managed to catch Lily smiling. Addie smiled, too, and texted the woman that Judson and she would be home soon.

Judson took the turn to the ranch, and she spotted one of the ranch hands patrolling the fence that was next to a deep ditch. The other was in the backyard between the house and the barn. Addie appreciated the extra eyes, and guns, and made a mental note to thank Rory's brother for sending them.

Judson pulled to a stop directly in front of the house, parking the cruiser so that she was only a few inches from the bottom porch step. He didn't repeat his *move fast* order. No need. Addie knew what she had to do, and added to that, she was anxious to get inside and see the babies.

She threw open her door. Across from her, Judson did the same, and he barreled out of the cruiser. So did she. But she had made it up only four of the eight steps when the sound of a gunshot ripped through the air.

Chapter Seven

Judson had no trouble hearing that gunshot. Or seeing the bullet slam into the post right next to where Addie was standing. But before he could even shout out for her to get down, another shot came toward them. Then, another, with all three coming too damn close to Addie.

Hell, they were under attack.

Judson didn't look for the shooter. He'd do that later, when Addie was safe. If that was possible. But at the moment, any of those shots could turn out to be deadly.

He tried not to think of that and focused on what he could do. Staying low and using the cruiser for cover as much as he could, he drew his gun and scrambled toward Addie. Thankfully, she had already dropped down and was trying her damnedest to flatten her body against the steps, but the wood porch wasn't going to provide much protection.

"The babies," Addie called out.

Yeah, Judson had already considered them and everybody else in the house. It was wood, too, and the bullets could go through the walls. The shooter didn't seem to be interested in doing that, though, since all the shots were aimed at the two of them.

That was both good and bad.

Addie and he were the targets. No doubts about that. And they could keep the gunfire and attention on them by not trying to get into the house. If they did, that's almost certainly where the shooter would turn their attention.

A bullet skipped off the top of the cruiser, ricocheting heaven knew where and giving Judson a spike of fear and more adrenaline that he definitely didn't need. He just had to concentrate. Had to make this work so that everybody except the shooter got out of this alive.

"Get the babies and Etta Jean into the bathroom," Judson shouted to Rory when the deputy opened the front door.

"Bennie's doing that now," Rory replied, and then he had to immediately duck back inside when a shot slammed into the doorframe.

"Don't do anything to make the bullets come your way," Addie pleaded. "No shots in the house."

So, Addie had worked that out as well, that they needed to keep the gunman's attention solely on them. Judson only wished he were outside alone. That he was the sole target and that Addie was somewhere else.

Someplace safe.

More shots came, all of them hitting the porch posts. Despite the fact that the sun was setting and the light wasn't optimal for target shooting, their attacker had a decent aim, only missing the mark by a fraction, and that's why Judson had to move Addie now.

He caught the first part of her that he could reach, her foot. And even though it would likely give her a few bruises and scrapes, he yanked her down the steps toward him.

Not a second too soon.

Because the shooter finally got the angle right, and the next bullet slammed into the spot where Addie had just been.

Judson dragged Addie closer to the cruiser and silently

cursed that she hadn't left the door open so they could dive inside. Of course, she hadn't known there'd be an attack. But he sure as hell should have anticipated it and done a better job of stopping her from being in harm's way.

"Who's doing this?" he heard her say over the loud, thick blasts.

"Don't know yet," he had to admit, and then Judson focused on trying to pinpoint the shooter.

He could hear the shouts of the ranch hands who'd been guarding the place, and he hoped they'd taken cover as well. Judson was positive that neither of them was firing, but the shots were coming from the area at the front of the ranch near the fence.

Near the drainage ditch, too.

But not in it.

Judson had played there plenty enough times when he was a kid to know it was deep enough to conceal a shooter, but he was pretty sure the shots weren't specifically coming from there.

So, he waited. Listened. And all the while he prayed that he could get Addie out of this alive.

For now the best he could do was try to shield her with his body, so he rolled over her, shoving her right against the cruiser. "Get underneath it," he ordered.

Addie's gaze shot to his, and he saw exactly what he'd expected to see in her eyes. The fear. Yeah, it was there. But part of that fear was for him.

"You get underneath, too," she insisted.

"I will, later. After I've done some things."

That was possibly an outright lie. If they got the chance to stop or pursue the shooter, he would. But he couldn't even start doing that until he had Addie out of the direct line of fire. Of course, a bullet could still reach her, but it would make the shooter's job much harder.

"Later," he repeated, and to hurry things along, Judson used his body to muscle hers beneath the cruiser.

He tore his gaze from hers. Had to. And Judson also had to shove aside the hurricane of emotions roaring through him. The fury over this SOB's attempts to kill them. The danger the gunman had brought right to the ranch's doorstep, putting the babies in harm's way yet again.

Yes, he had to put all of that aside and try drowning out everything but the way the barrage of shots was slamming into the porch and cruiser.

And he finally thought he had the location.

There was an old barn just on the other side of the road, and while he couldn't actually see anyone, he figured their attacker was perched in the hayloft, shooting through the spaces between the boards.

Plenty of room for a sniper to slip the barrel of an assault rifle through one of them and start shooting.

It wouldn't have been hard for the gunman to get there, either, since no one lived in the house that was about fifty yards from the barn. The elderly owner had died three years earlier, and there was a battle going on to determine ownership. From what Judson had heard, none of those involved in the legal wranglings had visited the place in over a year.

Even though the shooter was out of range for him, Judson levered himself up enough to send a shot in the gunman's direction. He probably missed by a mile, but at least it caused a pause in the gunfire. But only a pause. The shots started right back up again.

And that gave Judson an idea.

"Text Rory," he told Addie. "I want him to get a message to the ranch hand by the fence. The hand needs to stay down, but if he's able, I want him to start shooting into the barn. Have him aim high."

That last part was a safety precaution so that someone who just happened to be driving by wouldn't get hit by friendly fire.

From the corner of his eye, he saw Addie send the text, and Judson fired at the barn again. And again. Since that was giving him the lull he needed, he kept it up until Addie got a response.

"Rory's texting the ranch hand now," she relayed. "And he says backup is on the way. Two of them will be heading to the barn."

Good. But Judson knew that backup couldn't just come charging in. They'd have to hang back, wait for an opportunity to go after the shooter.

It wasn't long, only a couple of seconds, before Judson heard a welcome sound: gunfire, but this time it was coming from the ranch hand. And unlike Judson, he was in firing range to put a permanent end to this SOB.

But he immediately rethought that.

If possible, he wanted the shooter alive. Alive and talking so that Addie and he would know why someone was trying to kill them.

Judson reloaded and added his own gunfire to the mix of the ranch hand's, and as he'd hoped, the shooter stopped firing. Maybe because some of the hand's bullets were tearing through the old wood of the barn. Judson still didn't see any movement from the hayloft area, but that didn't mean the guy had been hit. He could be just lying low, waiting for an opening to start shooting again.

In the distance, he heard the wail of police sirens. Neither Judson nor the ranch hand stopped firing. They both kept pulling the triggers until Judson finally saw something.

A blur of motion at the back edge of the barn.

He caught just a glimpse, but it appeared to be someone dressed in dark clothes. Clothes that blended with the twilight. One thing was for certain, though.

The SOB was running.

Escaping.

And Judson had to do something about that.

"Stay put," he warned Addie, but Judson didn't give her a chance to respond. Definitely not a chance to try to talk him out of what he was doing.

He leaped up and took off running.

"Hold your fire," he shouted to the ranch hand, and the man immediately stopped.

That cleared the way for Judson to pick up the pace to a sprint while he kept his gun gripped in his hand. Kept his attention on that blur of motion, too. If the man, or woman, turned around, Judson wanted to be able to take cover rather than be gunned down.

Running as fast as he could, Judson reached the road just as he saw the cruiser approaching the turn for the ranch. He paused only a second to make sure the driver, Livvy, wasn't going to plow into him. When she slowed, Judson bolted across the road, vaulting over the pasture fence.

And he kept running.

His heart was thundering now, and his pulse was crashing in his ears, but thankfully he had yet another slam of adrenaline. The mother lode of energy that got him to the barn in no time flat.

He had to slow again, though, as he approached the barn. Slow down and keep watch in case this idiot tried to ambush him.

But he didn't see any signs of that. No signs of the shooter, either.

Not at first, anyway. Not until Judson picked through the darkness and saw the figure racing past the house. Clearly, the shooter had gotten some adrenaline, too, because within a blink, the person was out of sight, disappearing into a cluster of trees in front of the house.

Judson got moving, racing toward the snake. He was still a good twenty yards away when he heard a different sound. Not gunfire. But an engine.

He kicked up the pace again, trying to get to the shooter, trying to stop him before he escaped.

But he was too late.

Judson caught sight of the taillights as the car sped away.

Chapter Eight

Addie sat in the rocking chair in her bedroom, a sleeping baby nestled in each arm, while she waited for Judson. Waited and tried not to give in to the sickening dread that just wouldn't let up.

So much dread.

For the babies. For the danger they'd been in during the attack. For the possibility that the attacks weren't over, and that the gunman could strike again.

Yes, that was the fear all right, and Addie was hoping that Judson might be able to steady her nerves and give her some much-needed assurance once she was able to talk to him. She hadn't managed to have more than a couple of seconds with him before he'd run off toward that barn and the person who'd been firing those shots.

She knew he was busy with the aftermath of the attack. So were Rory, Bennie and Livvy. Rory and Bennie were staying close to the house in case the worst happened and the shooter returned, but Livvy and Eden were out looking for the person who'd tried to kill Judson and her.

Kill.

That was definitely a word, and a dread, that wasn't going away anytime soon. The shooter had been very determined to finish them off. Nearly had, too. And it was beyond frustrating that they still had no idea why this was happening. That was one of the big answers that Judson and the other cops were trying to find, and if they managed to catch the shooter, that would the start of getting answers.

In the meantime, they all had to take precautions. That included keeping the curtains drawn so a sniper couldn't pinpoint their location. There'd be no going outside for Etta Jean, the twins or her. Basically, they'd be prisoners in their own home while Judson and so many others were risking their lives. That didn't sit especially well with Addie, but priority one was the babies, and she had no intention of leaving them until this shooter was caught.

"Want me to help put the babies down?" Etta Jean asked.

That yanked Addie out of her doom-and-gloom thoughts, and she welcomed the reprieve. She glanced at Etta Jean, who was perched on the edge of a chair in the sitting area of the bedroom. Clearly, she was battling nerves and dread, too, but she seemed to be holding it together. So would Addie, for the sake of the twins. But she still wanted to see Judson.

Addie shook her head. "I want to hold them just a bit longer." She snuggled her face against Rose's baby curls and drew in that wonderful scent. "Thank you for protecting them," she added to Etta Jean, and she voiced something that she'd been afraid to say. "Were Lily and Rose scared during the shooting?"

All that noise had to be terrifying. Or rather, it had been for Addie. Because any of those shots could have gone into the house.

"I don't think so," Etta Jean replied after a slight hesitation. "Lily was crying, but I think that's because I gave her a jolt when I scooped her up, ran into the bathroom and climbed into the tub with her. She'd been sleeping," she explained. "Rose was awake, and Bennie was right by her bassinet, talking to her. She didn't fuss when he took her and followed Lily and me."

Addie's imagination was far better than she wanted. She could see all of that playing out. Lily crying. The sheer terror that Etta Jean and Bennie had to have been feeling as they put the babies in the tub and no doubt protected them with their own bodies.

Judson had done that for her. He had shielded her by having her move under the cruiser while he'd stayed in the line of fire. Addie hated that he'd done that. Hated that he had put her life ahead of his. But she was beyond thankful that neither of them, nor the ranch hands, had been shot.

Addie's head whipped up when she heard footsteps, and she tried not to show her disappointment when it wasn't Judson who stepped into the doorway but Livvy.

"Judson will be here soon," Livvy volunteered, letting Addie know that she obviously hadn't succeeded in hiding the disappointment. "He's finishing up giving his statement to Grace. I just wanted to drop by and check on you before I head back to the station."

"Any signs of the shooter?" Addie asked, already knowing the answer. If they had found him or her, then Livvy would have led with that.

Livvy shook her head, the frustration all over her face. "But the CSIs are in the barn, looking for anything that might clue us in to who fired those shots." She glanced at the babies and then at Etta Jean before her attention went back to Addie. "How's everybody holding up?"

Addie decided to go with a lie. "Okay." Because if she said that lie enough, she might start to believe it. Or better yet, it might start to be true.

Livvy made a sound to indicate she didn't quite believe

that, but she didn't push and then went for a change of subject. "The cops who notified Courtney's parents about her death said they were ripped to pieces, but they were able to give them some info. Apparently, Courtney talked to them a lot about Yvette, and there was plenty of bad blood between the women. Over the years Yvette has filed more than a hundred complaints against Courtney."

"That many?" Addie shook her head. "For what?"

"Lots of things. Yvette apparently liked to follow Courtney, so she's reported her for everything from speeding to jaywalking to littering. Yvette has even contacted plenty of Courtney's clients, trying to get them to have the woman fired or file a joint lawsuit against her."

It took plenty of anger for Yvette to do something like that. But then, the woman did blame Courtney for losing custody of Shane and Jennifer, and that was motive for murder. Not just for Yvette, but maybe for Jennifer and Shane, too. Jennifer might not have good things to say about her bio mom, but that didn't mean she wouldn't feel compelled to protect her in some way.

"Has the lab found anything in Courtney's car or on her clothes to link her to Yvette?" Addie asked.

"No." Livvy sighed again. "But it's getting priority treatment, so we might have something soon."

Livvy didn't add more, probably because she heard more footsteps coming up the hall toward them. And this time, it was the person Addie wanted to see.

Judson.

He stepped around Livvy, walking straight to Addie. He gave the twins a long look over before his gaze met hers. "We should talk. Are Lily and Rose ready for bedtime?"

Addie silently groaned. She didn't want to hear more

bad news, but she also didn't want Judson keeping anything from her, either.

"Yes, they're ready for bed," Addie muttered.

And they were. Despite everything, or maybe because of it, Etta Jean and Addie had already gotten them bathed and fed. They were wearing their footed pj's with Lily in her usual pink and Rose in yellow.

Judson eased Rose from her left arm, taking her to her bassinet while Addie did the same to Lily.

"I'll stay with them while you talk," Etta Jean said, making the same offer she had earlier that day.

That day, Addie mentally repeated. Had it only been that morning when the babies had gone missing? It felt like a couple of lifetimes ago. And while the day was technically over, the night certainly wasn't. With the gunman still at large, that wouldn't make for restful sleep.

Addie thanked Etta Jean and added a hug that lingered for several moments when she felt the tension in the woman's muscles. It was going to take them all a while to get past the trauma of what had happened.

"Call me if you need anything," Livvy offered as Judson and Addie went to the door.

"I will," Addie assured her and gave Livvy a hug, too. "And thank you for everything."

"Anytime," Livvy replied, and she walked away.

Judson took hold of Addie's hand and led her in the opposite direction. Not toward the front of the house, where there was so much chatter and activity still going on. He took her to the kitchen. When they found Bennie and one of the ranch hands there, Judson made a detour to the small sewing room that had once been the maid's quarters when the house was first built, over a hundred years ago.

The moment they were inside, he shut the door. And Judson pulled her into his arms.

Addie welcomed it. Mercy, did she. She needed this, and even though it brought on the inevitable heat, she didn't care. She just held on and let his arms ease some of the tight tension in her body. Only after she'd steadied herself did she say what had been flashing like neon lights in her head.

"You could have been killed," she blurted. "You put yourself between a shooter and me, and you could have died."

Judson had an odd reaction. The corner of his mouth lifted into a smile. It only added character to that amazing face that had way more character than a man had a right to have.

"I would tap my badge to remind you I'm a cop," he drawled. "But if I move my hand between us now, I might end up touching something of yours that I shouldn't."

For some stupid reason, that made her smile, too. It didn't last. But the old attraction came, and parts of her were certain she would enjoy Judson touching her. Well, if it weren't for the fact they'd nearly died and were in the middle of hunting for a killer.

"You wanted to talk," she managed to say, hoping it would get her mind back on track.

But she was instantly sorry for the change in subject. His smile vanished, and she saw the cop standing in front of her. A cop who eased back from her.

"Here's the bottom line," he started. "We don't know squat about who fired those shots. There are no visible tracks and so far none of the recovered shell casings have had fingerprints on them."

Her heart sank. She had been hoping that the CSIs or deputies would find something.

"You got a look at the shooter," she reminded. "Could it have been one of our suspects?"

"I got a couple of glimpses," Judson corrected. "And, yes, it could have been Elijah, Shane, Trevor or, hell, even Yvette. The only person it couldn't have been is Jennifer. She was at the police station at the time of the attack."

True. Jennifer had an airtight alibi, but that didn't mean Elijah hadn't been acting on her behalf.

"Elijah was furious when he left the station," she pointed out. "He could have fired those shots to get back at us for not letting him see Jennifer. Or he could have done this to try to make it seem as if she's innocent, that we're looking at the wrong person for Courtney's murder."

"Yes, he could have done it for either of those reasons, and trust me, Grace will be talking to him about that. To Shane and Trevor, too, when they come in for interviews in the morning." He paused. "You'll hear this soon enough, but all of our suspects have had firearms training."

Sweet heaven. It twisted at her to think of how easy it would be for one of them to try to come after them again.

"I don't want to leave the ranch," Addie said. "I want to be with the babies, but I want them to be safe."

Judson sighed and moved closer to her again. Not hugging her, but he did take her hand. "This all started with someone abducting the twins. The shooting today could have been another attempt to do that."

Oh, God. She hadn't even considered that. Those shots had been aimed at Judson and her, so Addie had assumed this was some sort of retaliation. But it could have been to eliminate them.

"We're beefing up security around here," he spelled out, obviously noticing the fresh round of fear in her eyes. "It's too risky to bring in someone from a security company right now, since we can't be sure our attacker won't use that as a chance to sneak onto the grounds. But the ranch hands will continue to patrol, and we'll keep all windows and doors locked."

She shook her head. "Is that enough—"

"And I'm sleeping in the room with you and the twins tonight," Judson interrupted.

"All right," she said, noticing his tone and body language. The muscles in his jaw were having a battle with each other. "You don't sound especially pleased."

Judson opened his mouth, closed it. Then sighed and cursed. "I'm doing it. I want to stay here and protect all three of you." He paused. "But I'll admit that it won't be easy."

She knew what he meant. What he felt. Because she was feeling the same exact things. All this close contact was testing those barriers again. It was tearing the pact to shreds. But at the moment she was having a hard time remembering why that would be such a bad thing.

And that's why she leaned in and kissed him.

She immediately felt the jolt. A sizzle of heat like electricity firing through her. It was always this way with Judson. So intense.

So hot.

But somehow it also managed to feel both wrong and right at the same time. *Damn pact.* They'd made that pact for good reasons, but those reasons and pretty much all logic went out the window whenever they kissed.

For now, Addie just settled on the part that felt right. The heat. The pleasure of his mouth and taste that set her on fire. Judging from the moan that came from deep within his throat, he was feeling the same thing.

He didn't throttle back. Didn't try to cut the kiss short.

Just the opposite. The kiss became hotter, and he slid his hand to her waist. Definitely what her body wanted. His touch coupled with the kiss. And that's what she got.

Judson kept his hand in place for a couple of heartbeats before he hooked his arm around her back and drew her to him. So close. With a lot of him touching a lot of her.

That amped up the heat even more, and Addie felt herself sinking deeper and deeper into that fire. She wanted to give in to it. Give in to Judson. She wanted to drag him off to bed. But thankfully there was just a sliver of reasoning coming through in her foggy brain, and that reasoning started to tick off why sex couldn't happen.

And it had nothing to do with the pact.

The house was full of cops, and there was an intense search going on. Even if they could be sure they'd have some uninterrupted time to sneak off to a bed, or the floor, it wouldn't be right. They needed to be helping with the investigation so they could stop any further threats.

Judson must have remembered that, too, because he tore his mouth from hers and stepped back. What he didn't do was curse or show any signs that the kiss had been a huge mistake.

Just the opposite.

Addie thought he might be on the verge of saying something about putting this on hold, but he didn't get a chance to actually voice that. Or anything else, for that matter. Because his phone rang.

"It's dispatch," he relayed to her, and he put the call on speaker.

Addie appreciated that. She didn't want to be kept in the dark about anything, but she tried to steel herself up since any contact from the dispatcher or his fellow cops could be another round of bad news.

"Judson, I've got someone on the line who wants to talk to you," the dispatcher said.

"Who is it?" he asked.

"She won't say, but she insists she had to talk to you. I can try to push her on giving me her name. Or I can have her contact Grace. You know we always get crackpot calls when there's any kind of investigation going on."

Judson made a sound of agreement, and his forehead bunched up while he no doubt considered what to do. "Put the call through," he finally said.

It took only a couple of seconds for the dispatcher to do that, and before Judson could get out a greeting, the woman's frantic voice poured through the room. "I tried to save those babies. I swear, I tried to save them."

Addie's chest went tight. But then she made herself remember that this could be a hoax.

"Who is this?" Judson demanded.

"Yvette Cates," the woman blurted.

Judson and Addie exchanged a glance, and his was tinged with some skepticism. "There's an APB out on Yvette Cates, and there are a lot of details about her on social media—"

"I'm Yvette," she insisted. And she began to rattle off details like her birth date and those of her two kids. Then she added, "My kids' names are Jennifer Alise and Shane David."

That seemed to convince Judson that she was telling the truth. And it caused the tightness in Addie's chest to increase. They were talking to the woman who had kidnapped the twins. Before Addie could blurt out a demand as to why Yvette had taken those precious babies, Judson voiced a demand of his own.

"Where the hell are you?" he snapped while he hit the

record function on his phone. He also sent a text to dispatch to try to have the call traced.

"I'm not sure, but as soon as I can, I'll get to a police station so I can give them my statement. Just promise me I won't be arrested."

Judson huffed. "I'm not promising that. You kidnapped two infants and endangered them—"

"No, I was trying to stop them from being hurt," Yvette insisted.

The woman was sobbing now. And whispering. Was she doing that so she wouldn't be overheard? If so, why?

Addie listened for any background noise. For any signs of a possible threat. But no one was shouting at Yvette or firing shots at her.

"The only person who put the twins in danger was you," Judson argued. "Now, tell me where you are."

Yvette did more sobbing before she spoke again. "Someone was going to take them," she said as if choosing her words carefully. "So, I took them first. I tried to get them to safety."

The skepticism skyrocketed big-time in Judson's eyes. "Who was going to kidnap them?"

"I… I can't say. Just believe me when I tell you that I was doing what I thought best. Are they all right?"

Judson seemed to debate his answer, or else he was stalling with the hopes of getting the call traced. "I can give you an update about them when I see you. Where are you?" he repeated.

Yvette didn't answer. Not with words anyway. But seconds later, there was a sound.

A bloodcurdling scream.

And the line went dead.

Chapter Nine

Judson stood in the shower in Addie's bathroom, hoping the hot water would perform some kind of magic. And fast.

He needed the cobwebs clear from his head. Cobwebs caused by the lack of sleep since he hadn't managed more than a couple of hours throughout the night. Hard to sleep while worrying about Addie and the twins' safety. Also, by being in the same room with her, mere feet away.

Yeah, that hadn't been easy.

His body hadn't let him forget how close she was or the lingering effects of that kiss they'd shared. Nope. No forgetting that. It was just as powerful as the other things going on in his mind and body.

Including the flashbacks.

Not just of the attack against Addie and him but also the call from Yvette. He could still hear the sound of her scream echoing through those cobwebs. It had seemed genuine. Like the woman had been terrified for her life.

But there was a problem with that.

They didn't know where Yvette was because they hadn't been able to trace the call. So, if she had indeed been screaming because of some horrible threat, her attacker could already have killed her and silenced her for good.

Being a cop all these years had made him enough of a

cynic to believe this was all some ploy to make herself appear innocent. It wouldn't work. If Yvette was alive and they could find her, she was going to pay for what she'd done.

Judson heard the dinging sound of a text, so he got out of the shower and glanced at his phone on the vanity. It was from Grace, updating him on the schedule. It wasn't his boss's first text of the day. She had sent one an hour earlier to let him know that Shane's and Jennifer's interviews were still on for the morning and that she'd be talking to the ME about Courtney's autopsy.

Yeah, plenty going on, but so far, they still didn't have the answers they needed to get a break in the investigation.

Judson texted back a thumbs-up emoji to Grace and gulped down the rest of the mug of coffee that he'd taken into the bathroom with him. Not his first cup, despite it being barely 8:00 a.m. He'd had that first one as he sat with the twins while Addie showered, and as soon as he made it back to the kitchen, he'd be tanking up on yet more caffeine.

He dressed in the clean clothes that Livvy had had brought over, putting on his holster and weapon, before he went into the bedroom. Addie was right where he'd left her, in the rocking chair with Rose. The baby had finished her bottle, though, and Addie was burping her.

"I heard your phone," Addie said, the worry in her eyes.

Of course, the worry had been there since the start of this ordeal, and sadly, it likely wouldn't be going away anytime soon.

"It was a text from Grace," he explained, going to the bassinet to check on Lily. She was still sacked out. "Trevor is on his way here. Grace decided to do the interview with him here rather than the police station. This way, she doesn't have to split the manpower and we can continue to show a strong police presence here."

"In case of another attack," Addie finished for him.

Judson had to make a sound of agreement. "Right now, there are three cruisers parked out front and four cops inside the house. Grace, Livvy, Bennie and me. The shooter might think twice before trying to come at us again."

Addie no doubt mentally played out what would happen later today. Grace, Livvy and Bennie couldn't stay here indefinitely, and the shooter could just wait for an opening. The danger wasn't over and wouldn't be until the killer and/or their attacker was caught.

"Trevor will be thoroughly searched before Grace allows him to step foot inside," Judson explained. "And she's going to ask if he'll submit to having his vehicle searched as well."

If Trevor refused, then Grace would get a search warrant. Trevor wasn't automatically guilty by association with his kidnapping wife, but simply being married to her should be enough to convince a judge that the cops needed to take a harder look at the man.

"Did Grace say anything about Yvette?" Addie asked in a whisper.

Judson shook his head. "No update on her."

Because they hadn't been able to trace the call, they had no idea where the woman was. Basically, they had to wait for Yvette to call them again. Or for someone to spot her.

Or for her body to turn up.

Despite the hell that Yvette had put Addie through by abducting the twins, Judson didn't wish the woman dead. Just the opposite. They needed Yvette alive and talking, especially if she'd been telling the truth when she claimed she had taken the babies to try to protect them.

That claim had cost Judson some sleep and was even

now going through his head. It was too bad Yvette hadn't spilled more info and named names. And Judson had given that some thinking time, too. Yvette likely would have been reluctant to rat out her own kids and her husband, so who did that leave?

Courtney?

There was no proof whatsoever that the social worker had wanted to kidnap the twins. And that no proof applied to anyone else. There hadn't been any threats and there wasn't any chatter on the dark web about abducting the babies. Of course, that didn't mean such a threat hadn't existed, but at the moment, everything still pointed to Yvette as the perpetrator of the crime.

Addie sighed, drawing his attention back to her, and she got to her feet. Like her sister, Rose was sleeping, too, and she didn't even stir when Addie eased her into the bassinet.

"What about Jennifer and Shane?" she asked, still whispering. "Please tell me they didn't disappear."

It was a valid worry, since Grace had cut both of them loose for the night. For Shane, there'd been no grounds to hold him, and his lawyer had put up enough fuss for Grace to allow Shane to leave with the promise he would return to the station in the morning to answer more questions.

Jennifer's situation had been different since she had been found at the scene with a knife and Courtney's blood, but there was still no evidence that she'd been the one to attack Courtney. In fact, the lab hadn't been able to find any of Jennifer's DNA on Courtney or in her vehicle. It was enough for Grace to allow the woman to leave—again with the stipulation that she return for an interview.

"They haven't disappeared," Judson assured her, but he didn't get a chance to add more because there was a soft tap at the door.

"It's me," Etta Jean said.

Since the door was locked, Judson crossed the room to let the woman in. Like Addie and him, there was plenty of fatigue and stress on Etta Jean's face, too, and she was carrying two mugs of coffee.

"I figured you could both use this," she immediately said, handing the mugs off to them. "There's also plenty of breakfast stuff in the kitchen. I made some bacon, eggs and biscuits and left it all warming on the stove."

"Thanks," Judson said after he'd gulped down some of the coffee.

He was sure his fellow cops and the ranch hands would appreciate the food. He would, too, since he'd need to fuel up to help with the fatigue, and he might be able to convince Addie to eat something as well.

"I'll stay with the babies as long as needed," Etta Jean added. She paused. "Any idea when we'll know…something?" she settled for saying.

Judson had to shake his head. "But there'll be at least three interviews this morning, and we might get something from one of those."

Etta Jean nodded, sighed and patted his arm. "Let me know the second you learn anything."

He assured her that he would, and Judson got Addie moving out of the bedroom and toward the kitchen. Apparently, others had had the same notion of fueling up and grabbing coffee, because they stepped in to find Grace and one of the ranch hands, Ty Matheson.

"Morning," Grace greeted, stepping to the side to make room for them at the stove. "How are you holding up?" she asked Addie.

Addie made a so-so motion with her hand. "The twins slept well enough."

"But not you." Grace sighed. "Eat up, because you're going to need it. We have a long day ahead of us." She was chowing down on a biscuit that she'd stuffed with bacon and scrambled eggs. "Trevor's ETA is fifteen minutes," she tacked on to that.

Not much time, so Judson made two of the breakfast sandwiches and handed one to Addie. Grace motioned for them to sit at the massive kitchen table.

"I didn't put it in the text, but the background report came through on Elijah," Grace started. "This will probably come as a surprise, but the man has no criminal record."

It was indeed a surprise. "His hot temper hasn't gotten him into legal trouble," Judson commented.

"Oh, it has," Grace corrected while Judson and Addie both took a bite of their sandwiches. "He was detained after a bar fight a year ago, but no one pressed charges after he agreed to pay for the damages. Elijah doesn't come from money or have a huge settlement like Yvette," she added. "Nor does he have a high-paying job. Still, he somehow managed to come up with the cash."

"Maybe he got it from Jennifer?" Judson suggested, washing down his sandwich with more coffee.

Grace lifted her shoulder. "Possibly, but she's not exactly rolling in dough, either. In fact, both Elijah and she are pretty much broke."

"Which could be motive for kidnapping babies," Addie piped in. "Yvette said she took the twins to protect them." She stopped, shuddered. "Maybe she was protecting them from Elijah."

"It's possible," Grace admitted. "Elijah doesn't have an alibi for, well…anything related to the investigation. Not for the kidnapping or for the attack. So, he could have planned to take the twins for ransom, thinking either you or Yvette would pay it."

During those sleepless hours of the night, Judson had considered that. And more. "If Elijah planned to abduct Lily and Rose for a payout, there would have likely been easier targets. Targets closer to his home, anyway. So, maybe this wasn't about getting a ransom. Maybe it was about getting his hands on Yvette's settlement money."

Addie was quick to mutter an agreement. Obviously, she'd done some nighttime thinking about this as well.

"If Elijah made Yvette believe he was going to take the twins," Addie spelled out, "then he could have been hoping that Yvette would steal them herself and that she would perhaps be killed or at least incarcerated in the aftermath. Then, he'd be a big step closer to getting his hands on Yvette's money either through receiving a ransom demand or convincing Jennifer to hand it over to him."

She stopped, sighed. And Judson knew why.

"Elijah would have had an obstacle or two, or three, to flat-out inheriting the money," Judson spelled out. "Trevor, for sure. Also, Jennifer and Shane. I can't imagine Trevor or Shane just giving him Yvette's money the way that Jennifer might."

"Same," Grace said. "And it's why I'm trying to get a copy of any will that Yvette might have. That might give us some answers."

Yes, it could, but it was a shame they couldn't question the woman herself.

"Are we certain there's actually money?" Addie asked. "I mean, we know Yvette received a settlement, but could she have already spent it?"

Grace shook her head. "There's money. I got her financials, and Yvette has every penny of it stashed in CDs. She hasn't tapped into any of it, and it's accumulating a nice chunk of interest each month."

That was indeed motive, then, for Elijah, Jennifer, Shane or Trevor. But motive didn't mean any of them had actually done anything wrong. In fact, the only guilty person was Yvette. An eyewitness had put her with the babies, and the woman had confessed to taking them.

And that brought Judson to more of his late-night thoughts.

"Yvette could have orchestrated it all," he said. "The anniversary of losing her kids is coming up. Along with it being their birthday, that could have triggered something in her. Or if she's using drugs, she might have become delusional, thinking that the twins were actually hers. She could have taken them and then gotten cold feet about what she'd done."

"Yes," Addie said, taking up the explanation. "After she left the babies with the farmer, she possibly could have rushed home to get things to make an escape and then run into Courtney."

Grace nodded. "If Yvette killed her, then the attack and that phone call could be about covering her tracks. If she could pin all of this on someone else, like Elijah, for instance, then she could walk away a free woman."

That would wrap everything up in a neat little package. Or rather, it would have been neat if they actually had Yvette.

Judson heard some voices at the front of the house, and at the same time, Grace got a text. "Trevor's here, and he's being frisked," Grace relayed to them, already getting to her feet.

She stopped and seemed to be considering how to handle this. "Why don't the two of you come with me to *greet*

Trevor? If Yvette didn't stage that attack on you, then maybe Trevor did. I'd like to see how he reacts to seeing you."

Judson wanted to see that as well. Too bad he couldn't hook Trevor up to a lie detector or dose him with truth serum, but he was at least hoping he'd get some kind of vibe from the man. Because if Yvette had enlisted anyone for help, it would likely be the man she'd married.

The three of them left their coffee and breakfast and headed toward the foyer, where Judson immediately saw Bennie, Livvy and a beefy man in jeans, a white muscle tee and a brown leather jacket that was almost the same color as his hair. Judson knew from the bio he'd read on Trevor that he was forty-nine, but he looked at least a decade younger than that.

"No weapons," Bennie announced.

Livvy added, "And I've given him the Miranda." Livvy also made introductions.

Trevor didn't acknowledge anything that Livvy or Bennie said. Nor did he look bothered about being frisked and treated like the suspect that he was. Instead, Trevor's attention was on Addie.

"Addie," the man finally said, aiming his weathered blue eyes on her. "I recognize you from the media reports," he quickly added when he must have noted the alarm on Addie's face. "I'm so sorry. I can't believe Yvette would have taken those babies from you."

So, the man wasn't going to defend his wife and proclaim her innocence. Interesting.

"Have you heard from Yvette?" Addie asked, not bothering to address the man's comments.

Trevor sighed, shook his head. "No. And I can't find

her. None of her friends have heard from her, either." He stopped. "You don't remember me, do you?"

Addie pulled back her shoulders, practically coming to attention, and her gaze combed over his face. "I don't," she admitted after a long pause. "How do you know me?"

Trevor's mouth turned into a slight smile. "You were just a kid, and it was a long time ago."

"How do you know me?" she repeated, this time her voice a snap, when Trevor didn't continue.

The man's smile faded, but he kept his attention on Addie. "When you were four or five, I went out with your mother a couple of times. With Rowena."

Because Addie's arm was against his, Judson felt her muscles tense. "She's not my mother."

"Yes, of course," Trevor was quick to say. "I wasn't aware of that at the time. Rowena introduced you as her daughter, and I had no idea what she'd done. *Murder*," he added under his breath. A look of disgust tightened his face. "Trust me, I wouldn't have had anything to do with her if I had known the truth. I didn't find out until a year or two later when I saw it on the news."

Judson considered all of that, and he'd need to try to figure out if what happened back then had anything to do with what was going on now. It seemed a stretch since it would have been almost thirty years ago, but it was an eerie coincidence that Judson didn't like.

"Mr. Cates, do you understand the Miranda rights that Deputy Walsh recited to you?" Grace asked, clearly shifting the subject. Maybe because she could see how uncomfortable Addie was.

That got Trevor's attention, and he finally turned toward the sheriff. "You're the one who arrested my stepdaughter."

"I didn't arrest her," Grace was quick to point out. "However, she is being questioned. So is your stepson."

Trevor nodded as if he'd fully expected that. "Jennifer doesn't get along with her mother. And I'm certain she despises me." He stopped. "Did Jennifer do something to Yvette? Is that why no one has heard from her?"

"We did hear from her," Grace said.

The silence settled over the foyer, and Judson watched the alarm go through Trevor's eyes. "When?" he snapped. "Where is she?"

"I'm sorry, but I'm not at liberty to get into the details," Grace said. "But we'll talk about that during the interview. I've set that up in the formal dining room, if you don't mind."

"I don't mind," he muttered, almost absently. His focus was clearly still on the contact they'd had with Yvette. "What did my wife say?" Trevor asked. "Did you tell her I was worried sick about her?"

Again, Grace dodged the question and motioned for them to follow her. She started walking at a very slow pace toward the dining room.

Trevor muttered some profanity. "Yvette has to be terrified. I really need to talk to her. If you'll just tell me where she is—"

"So, is this your first visit to the Horseshoe Ranch?" Grace asked. Maybe it was more question dodging, or Grace could possibly want to learn if Trevor was familiar with the house and the grounds.

"My first," Trevor grumbled. They stopped outside the dining room, but none of them went in. Instead, he shifted back to Addie. "My wife's a very troubled woman. If you saw her or spoke to her, you'd know that."

"Troubled? How?" Addie questioned, sounding a whole lot like a cop.

Trevor certainly didn't jump to answer. He seemed to be calculating how to handle this. Maybe because he was worried that Yvette had said something incriminating about him.

"Losing her kids has stuck with her," he finally said. "It's an obsession for her."

"What do you mean?" Judson pressed. "She lost the kids years ago."

"And she's never gotten over it," Trevor insisted. He stopped, groaned and scrubbed his hand over his face. "Look, I love my wife, but I can't always understand why she does the things she does."

"Like kidnapping two babies?" Grace supplied.

After several more of those long moments, Trevor nodded. "It's as if she can't get past what happened. As if she needs to relive it, with the illogical hope that she can somehow change things."

Addie and Judson exchanged a glance, and he could see she was just as confused as he was. Judging from Grace's next question, she clearly was, too.

"Explain that," Grace demanded. "And then we can begin the interview and get all this and more on the record."

For a moment, Judson thought that would get Trevor to back down, to try to wave it all off. But he didn't. "Yvette is obsessed with reading everything she can about the Horseshoe Ranch," he said. "Random mentions in the press, for instance. She'll print out and save those articles."

That did seem obsessive, considering that Jennifer and Shane hadn't spent much time here before being adopted.

"Over the years, Yvette's contacted any and all parents who had kids who ended up here," Trevor continued. "She tries to talk to them about their experiences. A sort of therapy, I guess you could say. But most don't want her pushing them about stuff like that. They've moved on. Yvette hasn't."

"Did you ever try to get your wife help for this?" Grace asked. "Maybe have her see a counselor?"

"Yes," he said on a heavy sigh. "I've tried many times, but she always refuses to go."

"Yet you married her," Judson pointed out in case Trevor was exaggerating Yvette's mindset.

"I did because I loved her. Still love her," he amended. "But love doesn't blind me to her faults. To this obsession she has with the Horseshoe Ranch and her kids. And I'm worried all this now caused her to go over the edge. When I'm done here, I need to make a few more calls so I can try to find out where she is," Trevor added a heartbeat later.

"Who else could you contact that you haven't already?" Grace pressed.

Trevor lifted his shoulder. "Yvette has a file with the names and phone numbers of those people I told you about, and she's in touch with a lot of them. Parents who lost custody of their children. Especially mothers," he said, turning back to Addie again. "Like yours."

Everything went tight inside Judson, and he saw some of the color drain from Addie's face.

"What do you mean by that?" Addie asked. "Are you saying Yvette has been in touch with Rowena?"

"That's exactly what I'm saying," Trevor confirmed.

Addie made a soft sound, part gasp, part moan, but Judson figured there was nothing soft about what she was feeling right now. Just the mention of Rowena was enough to trigger some god-awful memories for her.

"Yvette visited Rowena in prison many times," Trevor

went on. "In fact, that's how I met Yvette. Apparently, Rowena mentioned me during one of those visits, and Yvette looked me up."

Judson was going to have to check into Trevor's relationship with Rowena, but that tidbit didn't mesh with anything Jennifer, Shane or Elijah had said about Trevor. Then again, the three of them might not know that Rowena and Trevor had once dated.

"Rowena," Trevor repeated, and he snapped his fingers as if recalling something. "I was leaving for my camping trip, and the last thing Yvette said to me was that she was on her way to visit her. It's possible that's where Yvette is now."

Chapter Ten

Addie felt as if someone had punched her. When this hellish ordeal with Yvette had started, she certainly hadn't expected Rowena to be added to mix.

"Come on," Grace told Trevor, leading him into the dining room. "Let's get all this on the record." She had him sit at the table and then went back to join Addie and Judson in the hall.

"This might not be true," Grace said, obviously noticing that Addie had gotten that gut punch. "Yvette could have made it all up. Or Trevor could be the liar. Just don't jump to any conclusions yet."

Too late. Addie had already made that jump, and she was coming up with a very disturbing possibility. Had Rowena been the one to spur Yvette into kidnapping Lily and Rose?

"First things first," Grace went on, shifting to Judson. "Call and find out where this Rowena is and if Yvette is with her."

Judson nodded and stepped to the side to make the call. Grace stayed with Addie and took hold of her shoulders, forcing her to make eye contact. "Tell me about Rowena. When's the last time you saw her?"

It took Addie a couple of seconds to drag in enough breath to speak. "I haven't seen her since I was six. But yesterday, she called to tell me she was dying and that she wanted to see me." She stopped, had to, because she got another of those punches. "Rowena could have set up the kidnapping as a way to force me to see her. She could have arranged for Yvette to bring the babies to her."

"I won't rule that out," Grace said, "but at the moment just focus on the details. If Rowena's in jail—"

"She's not," Addie interrupted. "She's been released and is in some medical treatment facility in San Antonio. Judging from the route Yvette was taking to escape with the twins, she could have been heading in that direction."

Grace cursed under her breath. "All right. I'll get someone out there right away to check on—" But she stopped when Judson finished his call and came back over to join them.

"I just spoke to the director at Serenity Springs Care Facility, where Rowena is a patient," Judson explained. "Yvette isn't there. In fact, Rowena hasn't had any visitors since she arrived two days ago."

That eased some of the knotted muscles in her stomach and chest, but Addie was nowhere near ready to relax. "Rowena and Yvette could have worked out the kidnapping when Rowena was still in jail. The two could still be in contact."

Grace's forehead bunched up while she glanced at Trevor. "Okay, let me do this interview, and then I'll drive to San Antonio and have a chat with Rowena."

The words had no sooner left her mouth than Judson's phone rang, and Addie saw the name of the treatment facility on his screen. That bad feeling returned with a vengeance.

Judson moved them farther away from the dining room,

no doubt so Trevor wouldn't be able to hear, and he took the call on speaker. "This is Deputy Judson Docherty," he said.

Addie expected to hear the facility director's voice, maybe telling them that Rowena escaped. But it wasn't.

It was Rowena.

"I understand you just contacted Serenity Springs about me," Rowena said, skipping any greeting. "I was in the room with the director when she got the call," she added. "Yvette isn't here."

"When's the last time you saw her?" Judson was quick to ask.

But Rowena certainly wasn't quick to answer. "I won't get into that over the phone, but I will tell Addie and you in person. I'll tell you anything you want to know."

Now, it was Addie who cursed, and it wasn't under her breath. "That's blackmail," Addie spat out.

"Yes, it is," Rowena readily admitted. "But I need to see you, and if this is the way I can make that happen, then I'll use it."

"This is Sheriff Granger." Grace spoke up, the anger rising in her voice. "I can charge you with obstruction of justice and aiding and abetting a fugitive. You'll be sent back to prison and take your dying breath there."

Rowena coughed. "You could do that, and then I'll take what I know about Yvette to the grave. I've got nothing to lose, Sheriff Granger, by staying silent, because no matter what I do, I'll be dead in a couple of weeks."

"Fine," Grace snarled. "I'll send someone from SAPD over there now to arrest you."

"Wait," Addie mouthed, not saying it aloud since she didn't want Rowena to hear it. "Mute your phone," she told Judson and didn't add anything else until he had done that. "I can go see her."

"You can't," Judson snapped just as Grace insisted, "No need. I'm calling her bluff."

"It's not a bluff," Addie muttered. "Her one and only goal is to see me, and she'll risk going back to jail to get a chance at that happening."

Grace groaned and did more cursing. "You don't have to do this," she told Addie.

"I know," Addie replied, but it didn't exactly feel like an option. "As long as Yvette is at large, the babies are likely in danger. Judson and me, too. Heck, anyone around us as well. If Rowena has any inkling of where we can find Yvette, then it's something I need to do."

Grace didn't look convinced. Judson certainly didn't, either. And while Addie was dreading this, dreading it all the way to her bones, she would do it for those precious babies. She'd face down the monster who'd killed her mother and kidnapped her and hopefully get the truth about Yvette.

"All right," Grace said after what felt like an eternity of hesitation. "The two of you go to San Antonio. And take Livvy with you."

Addie shook her head. "No. I want her to stay here. I want all the protection possible for Lily and Rose."

Grace shook her head, too. "I'll be here. So will Bennie and two of the ranch hands. But there's no way I'll send Judson and you out there alone without backup. Go and have Livvy follow in a cruiser. That way, if the killer sees two cop cars, he or she might think twice about launching another attack."

Addie wanted to argue with that, but then she remembered this wasn't just about her. Judson would go with her, she had zero doubts about that, and it meant he'd be in danger.

"All right," Addie agreed. She turned to Judson. "Can

we leave now? The sooner we get this done, the better. I don't want to sit around here thinking about it."

His expression morphed from deep concern to anger, which she didn't think was directed at her but rather Rowena. "Okay," he finally said. "But I stay with you during the visit. You're not doing that solo, even if Rowena insists on it."

Addie had no trouble agreeing to that. This visit would be beyond hard, but without Judson, it felt impossible. Besides, Judson was the cop, and this could serve as an official interview.

"Just let me give the babies a quick kiss goodbye," Addie insisted, hurrying toward her bedroom.

She stepped into the room and found them both asleep. Etta Jean was folding laundry on the bed, and she must have seen something in Addie's expression, because she immediately asked, "What's wrong?"

"I just have to visit someone," Addie settled for saying. "Judson's going with me. If you need anything, let Bennie or Grace know. And call me if there's any sign of trouble."

Etta Jean gave a shaky nod and kept her gaze pinned to Addie as she gave each baby a kiss on the cheek. Addie gave Etta Jean a hug, too, and then hurried back out to find Judson waiting for her at the door.

"The cruisers are ready," he let her know.

Clearly, he still wasn't convinced this was the right thing to do, but he didn't hesitate getting them out of the house and into the waiting cop car. Livvy was already in her vehicle, and they took off, heading toward San Antonio.

"Should I call the treatment center and let them know we're coming?" Addie asked.

"No. I don't want anyone there knowing our plans. Especially Rowena. She could call the person who attacked us."

Oh, mercy. Addie hadn't even considered that, but it was a possibility. Rowena had made it seem as if she'd wanted to say goodbye, but the woman could have something sinister in mind.

Like trying to kill Addie for rejecting her.

"If you want to change your mind about this visit, I can turn around and take you home," Judson offered.

"No." Addie steeled herself up and mentally repeated that a couple of times. "I want to find out anything Rowena knows about Yvette."

Judson's jaw muscles tightened, but he didn't turn around. However, he did keep watch around them as they headed toward the interstate, and he used a voice command to call the prison where Rowena had been an inmate. It took him several minutes to work his way to the warden.

"Curtis Sanchez," the man said when he came on the line.

"Deputy Judson Docherty from Renegade Canyon PD. I'm pressed for time, and I'm hoping you can help me. Rowena Matthews's name had come up as connected to a fugitive wanted for abducting two infants. Yvette Cates."

"Yes, I saw that on the news," Sanchez said, but then he paused. "How's Cates connected to Rowena?"

"It's possible they were friends. I need you to tell me if Yvette ever visited Rowena while she was incarcerated?"

"Hold on a second and I can check that." They heard the clicks of a keyboard in the background, and it didn't take long for the man to come back on the line. "Yes, she did. Lots of times. Three visits in the last two weeks. Before that, Yvette came about every other month."

So, something had caused those visits to increase. But what? Had the women been planning the trip to the

Horseshoe Ranch to get the twins, or was this about something else?

"Were the visits monitored?" Judson pressed. "In other words, were they recorded?"

"Supervised but not recorded," Sanchez admitted. "Rowena wasn't considered a flight risk. In fact, while she was here, she was a model prisoner, which was why she was granted medical release. Why? Do you think Rowena had a part in the abduction of those babies?"

"I'm not sure. What about other visitors?" Judson pressed. "I'm specifically looking at other parents who might have lost custody of their kids and were taken into care by CPS."

"Well, I wouldn't have that info, but I can send you a list of names of her visitors. Would that help?" Sanchez asked.

"It would. Text it to my phone, and I'll share it with my boss, Sheriff Granger. We can dig through the names and see if anything pops." Judson paused. "By the way, for what it's worth, Rowena isn't being a model citizen now that she's out," he explained. "She's refused to give the cops vital information about Yvette unless she speaks to the woman she abducted as a child. It's down and dirty blackmail."

"I'm sorry to hear that." And the man sounded genuine. "I can call and speak to her if you think that'll help."

Judson seemed to consider that and then said, "No, but thanks for the offer. I'll be in touch if I end up filing charges against her. Then, you can decide if you want to try to revoke her release."

The warden thanked him, and Judson ended the call. With the silence filling the cab of the cruiser, there was nothing to interfere with her thinking, and dreading, this face-to-face. Addie wouldn't change her mind, but she could feel the tension building, building…

And then it stopped when Judson took her hand and gave it a gentle squeeze. That was all it took to settle some of her raw nerves. All it took to lower that barrier between them another notch.

"Just think about the babies," Judson said, his voice oh so calm. "Think about holding them, feeding them." He paused. "Think about how many times they'll wake us up tonight." He grinned at her.

The moment seemed way too light, considering everything that was going on. But it also seemed intimate. And it was. After all, they might be sharing a bedroom again, and the intimacy between them was building, too.

It'd been years since they'd been lovers. A lifetime ago. Yet, all those memories came flooding back to her now. Of the hot kisses on the seat of his pickup truck. The touching. The need. So much need.

The making out had escalated until they'd finally done the deed. And repeated it throughout the summer right before he'd left for the military and she had left for college.

Sometimes, like now, she wondered what would have happened if they'd both stayed in Renegade Canyon. Would they have ditched the pact they'd made and hooked up for good?

Maybe.

And that's what Addie decided to focus on. That and her future with the babies. She let herself sink right into the images and stayed there until Judson drove into San Antonio and to the Serenity Springs Care Facility.

"It doesn't look like a prison," Addie remarked when she eyed the two-story redbrick building with the white columns. "Or a hospital."

It looked more like someone's home. An expensive one. And it seemed way too luxurious to house a killer.

Judson pulled to a stop in one the visitors' spots, and Livvy parked right next to him. He didn't get out. He turned in the seat to look Addie straight in the eyes.

"I'm not changing my mind," she let him know.

"I figured as much. I was going to say, don't let her get to you. Keep the conversation on Yvette and the present. Don't let Rowena drag you into the past."

It was good advice. Easier said than done, but still good, and that's why she leaned in and brushed her mouth over his. For the advice and because she knew, like his touch, the kiss would soothe her.

And it did.

It aroused her, too, but Addie figured she could embrace the heat while they made their way out of the cruiser and inside.

With Livvy right behind him, they stepped into the facility, and while the foyer didn't look much like a hospital, either, it smelled like one. That antiseptic smell seemed to coat everything from the high plastered ceilings to the marble floors.

Judson immediately went to the reception desk to deal with the woman in pale blue scrubs who certainly wasn't welcoming them. In fact, she seemed ready to send them on their way. Judson showed her his badge, followed by a murmured conversation.

The woman gave Addie a long look before she called someone, and she continued to scrutinize both Livvy and Judson while she spoke to whoever she'd called. Probably the director. Heck, maybe even Rowena.

After she ended the conversation, she typed in something on her laptop and used her phone to take a photo of Judson's badge. She also had him sign something before she finally stood.

"This way," she said. "The patient has agreed to see you."

Yes, Addie would bet Rowena had, and she was probably fist pumping in triumph at getting her way. The thought of that disgusted Addie even more.

The receptionist led them down a long hall and stopped outside a room across from a nurses' station. The nurse manning it was on the phone, and he barely spared them a glance before they went inside.

Definitely a hospital room.

Not just the scent but the bed and the equipment that surrounded it. And in that bed sat Rowena, looking considerably older than the last time Addie had seen her. Looking considerably older than her age, too. It was obvious the cancer had taken a toll on her, as her face was very thin. Her head was wrapped in a bandanna that had been fashioned into a cap.

"Addie," Rowena said, her voice a hoarse rattle. She lifted her hand and motioned for Addie to come closer.

She didn't.

Addie stayed put, and she didn't even attempt to soften her glare of disgust. That disgust went up a notch when she spotted the photo of herself on the nightstand. Definitely not one that Addie had given her, but rather one that had been printed out from an online newspaper article that had been done about the Horseshoe Ranch when Addie had taken over running it.

"Deputy Judson Docherty," he said, breaking the cold silence that had settled in the room. He hitched his thumb to Livvy. "Deputy Walsh. Now, start talking, Rowena," he added. Judson certainly wasn't toning down his venom, either. "Babies are at risk, and I don't want to waste a second with these sick mind games you're playing."

Rowena finally tore her stare from Addie and shifted to Judson while she shook her head. "No mind games. I needed to see my… Addie."

Even though the woman hadn't said the d-word, *daughter*, Addie knew she was thinking it. And that upped Addie's anger even more.

"I needed to say I'm sorry," Rowena went on, shifting her attention back to Addie. "I'm so very sorry for taking you, and while I don't expect your forgiveness—"

"Good," Addie snapped. "Now, tell us about Yvette so we can get the heck out of here."

Rowena sighed, and for a moment Addie thought the woman was going to keep the conversation on the past. But she didn't.

"I had no part in taking those twin baby girls," Rowena finally said. "I want you to know that up front. And I had no idea that Yvette would do it, either."

Judson put his hands on his hips and aimed narrowed eyes at Rowena. "You'd better tell us a hell of a lot more than that, or I'll be filing charges against you. I've already spoken to the warden, and he's considering revoking your release."

That put some alarm in Rowena's eyes, and she gave a shaky nod. "There's more. I just wanted you to understand that I didn't know what Yvette was going to do. If I had, I would have tried to talk her out of it."

Judson made a circling motion with his finger for Rowena to continue when she fell silent.

"Yvette started visiting me years ago," she went on. "She was furious that her kids had been taken from her, and she blames CPS and anyone connected with the Horseshoe Ranch." When her voice cracked, she reached for a container of water and had a few sips. "Recently, Yvette was worried that someone had been drugging her."

"Who?" Judson demanded.

"She didn't know, but she thought it might be Trevor. Or Jennifer's boyfriend, Elijah."

That got Addie's attention, and while she didn't go closer, she was very interested in this part of the conversation.

"Yvette thought Trevor or Elijah might be trying to kill her so they could get their hands on her money," Rowena added.

"Did she have any proof?" Judson pressed.

Rowena shook her head and sighed. "And I'm not sure it was actually happening. Yvette seemed to be having some kind of breakdown. I think maybe because of the rift between Jennifer and her. She loves her daughter very much, and it was tearing her apart that Jennifer was being so hostile."

Addie kept up the glare and intensified it when Rowena looked at her. The woman was clearly applying Yvette's situation to her own.

Or trying to, anyway.

Addie wanted to blurt out a reminder that Rowena was a killer and a child abductor and deserved hostility, but she didn't want to give this woman anything. Not her words, not her anger. Not her attention. And that's why Addie shifted her gaze to a spot on the floor. No more eye contact.

"Is that it?" Judson asked. "Did you drag us all the way out here for that?"

"There's more," Rowena was quick to say. "Shane also believes Trevor could have been drugging his mother. If he was, then maybe Trevor used the drugs to manipulate Yvette into taking those babies."

"Wait," Judson said. "You've talked to Shane, or is this

hearsay from Yvette?" Addie definitely wanted to know the same thing.

"Not hearsay," Rowena insisted. "I've spoken with Shane plenty of times. At first, Yvette brought him with her when she visited me in prison. Then, later, Shane started coming alone."

Addie didn't like the sound of that. What would Shane have wanted with a convicted killer? It certainly wouldn't have been just to accompany his mother, since he'd done solo visits, too.

So, what had Shane been doing there?

Unfortunately, Addie could think of a reason. If Shane was angry about being placed into foster care, then he could have been thinking it was time for payback, against CPS and the Horseshoe. It chilled Addie to the bone to consider that was why Courtney had been murdered and the twins had been taken. Yvette and Shane could have come up with this sinister plan together.

But did Rowena play into that plan in any kind of way?

"I'm guessing Shane didn't have any proof that Trevor or Elijah was drugging Yvette?" Judson asked.

"No," Rowena replied. "But Shane despises both men and thinks they're after his mother's money. He said his mom and sister were weak and naive for getting involved with the likes of those two. He was also worried that Jennifer might try to get back at Yvette for the miscarriage."

"What miscarriage?" Judson snapped.

"Jennifer's." She paused. "You didn't know," she muttered. "Jennifer had a miscarriage last month, and she told Yvette that she believed the stress caused it. Stress her mother caused by being with Trevor."

Addie had no idea if that kind of anxiety could cause a woman to miscarry, but if Jennifer had believed that, it might be motive for her to get back at Yvette in some way. But there were a lot simpler ways to do that than threatening to kidnap the twins and spurring Yvette to try to "rescue" them.

"The last time Shane and I spoke," Rowena went on, "he was trying to convince Yvette to cut Trevor and Jennifer out of her will. He thought if Jennifer couldn't inherit, then there'd be no threat to Yvette from Elijah."

Addie considered that, and she could see Shane's point. That would eliminate possible threats if the two were indeed trying to get Yvette's money. But Shane could have also wanted Yvette to cut them out of the will so he could inherit it all.

"Any ideas where would Yvette be hiding out right now?" Judson asked.

"She usually just talked about her children and husband, but she did mention a fishing cabin that Trevor owns."

That was the place where Trevor had claimed to be during the twins' abduction. Addie knew from the updates she'd read that the cabin had already been searched, and there'd been no sign of Yvette.

"Anywhere else?" Judson asked when once again the woman fell silent.

"No. I'm sorry. Like I said, Yvette kept the conversation on her kids and what she'd gone through with CPS. I can't imagine she'd go anywhere without telling Shane, though. Yvette seemed very devoted to him."

Well, if Yvette had told Shane, he wasn't volunteering the info. Hopefully, though, that might change since both Jennifer and Shane could still be in interviews at the police station in Renegade Canyon.

"Is that it?" Judson asked. "You've got nothing else to tell us about Yvette or her husband and kids?"

More silence followed. "Nothing more about Yvette and Shane," Rowena finally said. "But I want to talk to Addie. Just give me five minutes so I can say my piece," she added in a plea.

That snapped Addie out of her thoughts about the investigation and gave her a cold, hard reminder of where she was. The anger came. Mercy, did it, and she had to clench her fists to stop herself from storming across the room and ripping up that photo of her.

But even that would be giving Rowena the attention that Addie didn't want her to have. In fact, she wanted to give this woman exactly what she deserved.

Which was nothing.

Absolutely nothing.

Without even sparing Rowena a glance, Addie turned and walked out.

Chapter Eleven

Judson didn't say goodbye to Rowena or thank her for talking to them. He was still way past being riled that the woman had forced Addie to go through this to give them those scraps of info. As far as he was concerned, those scraps had come at too high a price for Addie, and Rowena had put Addie through hell and back, all so she could see her.

Livvy and he followed Addie out of the room with Rowena calling out, "Addie. Just forgive me before it's too late."

Addie didn't respond. She just kept walking and only paused for them to catch up when she made it to the front door. Judson didn't linger. It was obvious that Addie needed to get the heck out of there now, so he scanned the parking lot of any signs of a threat. When he didn't see one, he hurried Addie out of the building and got her into the cruiser.

"Give me a second," she muttered while she gulped in some long, deep breaths. She was clearly trying to steady herself.

"Take all the time you need," he assured her.

Judson didn't touch her. Didn't pull her into his arms to try to comfort her—something he truly wanted to do. But he figured there was nothing he could say or do right now that would make this easier. So, he just sat quietly and waited her out.

Addie didn't cry, but she did mutter some ripe profanity under her breath. She also groaned and squeezed her eyes shut.

His phone sounded with a text, and he saw the message from Livvy pop up on the dash screen. On the drive back, I'll put more pressure on Yvette's lawyer to give a copy of her latest will.

Good. Judson sent her a thumbs-up emoji. Seeing the will would confirm if Yvette had indeed written her daughter and husband, Trevor, out of it. Of course, that didn't prove squat. Even if Yvette had basically disowned Trevor and Jennifer, they might not have even known about it. The will wouldn't necessarily be motive for drugging Yvette and pushing her to become mentally unstable.

But Yvette might not be the unstable one.

Jennifer could be, and while he hated to believe anything Rowena had just told them, he had to at least consider that Jennifer had indeed blamed Yvette for the miscarriage and that everything that'd happened in the past twenty-four hours had been orchestrated to get back at Yvette.

He considered texting Eden and Rory to find out if they'd learned anything in their interviews with Yvette's kids, but he dismissed that. If there was anything relevant, it'd soon be coming in a report. Something he'd need to do as well to fill Grace and the others in on the conversation with Rowena.

"You might think I should have just said I forgive her," Addie said, her voice cutting through his thoughts.

"I don't think that at all," he was quick to say. "Today proved that she's manipulative and self-centered. It was all about what she wanted, and she had no consideration for what a visit would put you through."

He saw some of the tension fade from her shoulders and face. "Thank you for that."

"Just stating the truth," he assured her, and because the timing felt right, he went ahead and pulled her into his arms.

Addie made a sound, sort of a sigh mixed with a soft sob, and she dropped her head on his shoulder. Judson tightened his grip around her, but he also kept watch. Making sure they weren't about to be attacked. He was certain Livvy was doing the same thing. Sitting here was a risk, but he wanted to give Addie these moments to try to settle from the emotional ordeal she'd been through.

"She is self-centered," Addie muttered. "And narcissistic. She made my life a living hell long before I even knew she'd murdered my mother and kidnapped me. I had to be perfect. My hair, my clothes, my manners. Everything. I had to present the perfect child to her so-called friends."

Over the years, Addie had mentioned bits and pieces of her life with Rowena. She'd been forced to perform in pageants, and Rowena had even put Addie on severe diets when she'd been only five years old.

"She was never violent with me," Addie went on. "She never physically hurt me the way she did my mother." The venom, and the hurt, spiked in those words. "But there was abuse."

Yeah, there had been, and while Judson hadn't wanted to pry into that part of Addie's life, once he'd become a cop, he had taken a look at the case file and reports after Rowena's arrest. Along with the diets and strict training routines for the pageants, Rowena had basically isolated Addie, not allowing her to make friends and even pulling her out of school so that Addie stayed right by her side. Rowena's generous inheritance from her late parents had allowed her to have that lifestyle.

And to basically keep Addie a prisoner.

Addie lifted her head and met his gaze. "Thank you," she said.

Judson felt he should be the one doling out the thanks for allowing herself to be put through this, but he didn't get the chance.

"Just please get me far away from her," Addie insisted. "I need to get back to the ranch and see Lily and Rose."

He needed that as well. Not just to put some distance between Rowena and them but because it was safer for Addie to not be out in the open like this. Plus, seeing the twins would settle both of them.

The moment they both had on their seat belts, he pulled out of the parking lot, and with Livvy behind them, they headed home. From the corner of his eye, he saw Addie text someone. Probably Etta Jean to let the woman know their estimated time of arrival.

Judson had barely made it out of San Antonio when his phone rang and Eden's name popped up on the screen. He went ahead and took the call on speaker, hoping this wasn't bad news.

"Should I ask how the meeting with Rowena went?" Eden said the moment she was on the line.

He waited and let Addie respond to that. "Rowena didn't give us any new info on where we might find Yvette, but she did mention the fishing cabin."

"She's definitely not there," Eden confirmed. "Well, not unless she showed up after the crime scene team left about an hour ago." She paused, and Judson heard what he thought was Eden texting someone. “I’m having one of the county deputies go back and have a look just in case.”

That was a smart move. Yvette had to be somewhere. Well, unless she was dead. And if she was alive, she might try to hole up in a familiar place rather than risk checking into a hotel.

“Did you get anything else from Rowena?” Eden asked.

Again, Judson let Addie take that question. “Nothing more on possible locations, but Rowena told us that both Yvette and Shane visited her in prison and that she believes either Trevor or Elijah are trying to eliminate Yvette so they can inherit her money.”

“Interesting,” Eden muttered. “During my interview with Jennifer, she pointed the finger at Trevor, too. And at her brother.”

No surprise there. If money was indeed the reason to get Yvette out of the picture, then Trevor, Shane, Elijah and Jennifer all had motive. But all these accusations were muddying the investigative waters. What they needed was proof.

“Did anything come out in Rory’s interview with Shane?” Judson asked Eden.

“Not really. Shane certainly didn’t mention anything about having visited Rowena,” she explained. “We had to cut Shane loose about a half hour ago, but we can call him and ask him about that.”

“I’ll do that,” Judson heard Rory say in the background.

Good. Because Judson wanted to hear what Shane had to say about those trips to the prison.

“What about Jennifer?” Judson asked. “Is she still there?”

“No. Grace said not to hold her, and we didn’t. She left shortly before her brother did. Elijah picked her up.”

Again, that wasn’t much of a surprise. Grace didn’t have

the evidence to arrest Jennifer, and of course, she would have wanted her boyfriend to get her the heck out of there.

"Did Jennifer say anything about her recent miscarriage during the interview?" Judson added.

"She did. Said it happened about six weeks ago." Eden paused. "Why? Is it important?"

"Could be." Judson stopped and decided to rephrase that. "According to Rowena, it's important, anyway. I don't have a clue if Rowena is telling the truth, though. If she is, then Jennifer blames her mother for creating the stress that caused her to lose her baby."

"Wow," Eden muttered. "That could be a game changer and maybe give Grace enough to make an arrest, since it speaks to motive."

Yes, it did, but Judson wasn't sure they'd be arresting the guilty party. "What was your gut feel when you interviewed Jennifer?" he asked Eden. "Do you think she could have done the whole deal? Drug her mother and provoke her into abducting the twins so she could get back at Yvette?"

"My gut feel is she probably couldn't have done it solo," Eden said on a sigh. "She's an emotional wreck, likely suffering from some lingering trauma from her miscarriage. FYI, during the interview, Jennifer said a couple of times that the baby would have made her relationship with Elijah stronger. When I pushed on that, I got the impression that she's worried he's about to dump her."

Judson was giving that some thought when Addie voiced a question that was forming in his own mind. "When did Elijah and Jennifer start seeing each other?"

"Shortly after Yvette was awarded all that money in her settlement," Eden admitted. "But that's also around the time Trevor and Yvette hooked up. The timing is so coincidental that I understand why Shane thinks they could be gold diggers."

Shane just might be right about that, too. "Grace should soon be finished interviewing Trevor," Judson commented. "What about Elijah? Is Grace bringing him back in, too?"

"Yep. This afternoon," Eden verified. "And Grace is already done with Trevor, and he's left the ranch. Grace is doing a report, but the gist is that Trevor didn't admit to any wrongdoing. He put it all on Yvette, and he swears up and down that he doesn't know where she is or why she took the twins."

Convenient, since the woman wasn't around to give her side of the story. But Judson was glad of one thing—that Trevor was no longer near the twins. It didn't matter that the man hadn't been armed, he was still a suspect, and Judson wanted him far away from Lily and Rose.

"Hold on a second," Eden muttered.

In the background, Judson heard Rory say something he didn't catch, but Eden relayed it a second later. "Rory wanted me to tell you that Shane didn't answer when he tried to call him. Rory left him a message."

Judson didn't care much for all their suspects being in the wind, again, but that only made him want to work harder to get to the bottom of what was going on.

He took the turn off the interstate, and since he'd made this trip so many times over the years, he knew they only had about ten miles before they made it to the ranch. If Grace was still there, he'd catch her up and then start diving into the reports of the interviews to see if there was some kernel of info he could use.

When he heard Addie draw in a quick breath, Judson glanced at her and saw that she was looking at the spot where they'd found the twins. Nan Fredrick wasn't at the end of the road today. No one was. But Addie must have gotten a jolt from the memory of what had gone on here.

Once they were past the farm road, Addie tore her gaze from it and looked at him. For only a couple of seconds, anyway. They seemed to spot the movement together as Judson rounded a curve.

A woman.

Hell. What was this? Some kind of trap or diversion so the killer could attack them? Maybe. But the woman was real. And there was blood on her face. Judson had no trouble seeing that or the fact she was running up the road straight toward them. In the distance he could see a black car in the ditch.

He hit the brakes, thankful that Livvy reacted quickly, too. If she hadn't, the cruiser would have slammed into them, and Judson might have hit the woman.

"Help me," she shouted just as a text lit up his dash.

I'm calling this in, Livvy messaged. Any idea who she is?

It was hard to tell with all the blood, but the car in the ditch was damn familiar. "I think it's Yvette," Judson said.

Addie made a sharp sound of surprise and moved to the edge of her seat, no doubt to get a better look. That look was made considerably easier as the woman continued to come closer.

Yeah, it was Yvette, all right.

And judging from the blood streaming down her face, she had some kind of head injury. Either that or she had staged this to make it look as if she was hurt.

Judson didn't open the door to her, not even when Yvette shouted, "Help me." But he'd soon have to do that if for no other reason than to take her into custody.

The woman was firing glances over her shoulder as if looking for anyone who might be following her. Judson couldn't see anyone, but that didn't mean an attacker wasn't in that ditch, waiting and ready to strike.

In case another vehicle came barreling toward them, Judson turned on his lights and siren. Behind him, Livvy did the same. That didn't slow Yvette. Not a first, anyway. But after another glance over her shoulder, she stopped and turned, her attention zooming toward a cluster of trees just off the road. Judson thought he saw the start of a trail there, too.

"Does she see someone?" Addie asked. "Or is this some kind of ploy?"

Judson didn't know, and he didn't have time to figure it out because there was a loud blast that he had no trouble recognizing.

A gunshot.

And it'd come from those trees.

Yvette screamed, a bloodcurdling sound that ripped through the air, and she dropped to her knees. Judson couldn't tell if she'd actually been shot, but he knew he had to do something. If Yvette truly was in a danger, she could be killed right in front of him.

"Get down in the seat and stay in the cruiser," Judson told Addie while he threw the car into Drive and moved up closer to Yvette.

It wasn't easy, since the road was so narrow, but he turned the cruiser sideways to make it easier to reach Yvette through the driver's side door. That wasn't a huge precaution, considering that someone had already tried to kill Addie and him, but it was better than him just bolting out where he could be gunned down.

Judson threw the cruiser into Park and opened his door. He drew his gun and automatically braced himself for the sound of another bullet.

But none came.

However, even over the sirens, he could hear Yvette moaning, and she was now clutching her chest.

Livvy moved her cruiser, too, parking so that she was right next to the passenger's side where Addie sat. Hopefully, Livvy would be able to protect her if things went to hell in a handbasket.

And they did.

Damn it, they did.

The gunfire blasted out from the trees. A spray of shots that slammed into the cruisers and the pavement. They would have likely slammed into Judson, too, had he not dropped down, using the front end of the cruiser for cover.

Judson considered leaning out, trying to pinpoint the shooter, but the bullets were coming too close to him. Pinning him down.

"Stay low," Livvy shouted a split second before Judson heard more gunfire.

From Livvy this time. And he cursed when he glanced behind him and saw that Livvy was behind her cruiser door and was returning fire. She only managed a couple of rounds before the shooter shifted his aim and sent some shots her way.

Cursing, Judson levered himself up and fired where he thought their attacker was, and he did some praying. Praying that Livvy and Addie weren't getting hit, since bullets could eventually get through both the window and the body of the cruisers. He also added a prayer that he could get Yvette out of this alive. Even if she was working with the gunman, she could give them answers as long as she wasn't dead.

But she wasn't screaming.

And she was moving.

Judson could see the blood spreading out from her, sliding across the pavement. There was way too much of it, and if he didn't do something soon, Yvette would bleed out.

"I'm driving closer to her," Judson let Livvy know.

He jumped back in the cruiser, giving Addie just a glance. He wanted to make sure she was all right, wanted to give her some kind of reassurance, but there wasn't time for that.

"Call for an ambulance," he told her. Not just to give her something to do, either. If he could get Yvette into the cruiser, they'd need EMTs out here right away.

Addie's hands were trembling when she took out her phone, but she made the call while Judson pulled up closer to Yvette. As close as he could get without hitting her. He aligned the back door with the woman and glanced at Addie again.

"Stay down," he repeated.

Just as a shot slammed into the window right above her head.

The glass cracked and webbed but held. Still, it could break at any second, and that's why Judson knew he had to move fast.

"All the way down in the seat," he told Addie, but she was already heading in that direction.

"You, too," she managed to say. She must have known, though, that wasn't something he could do. Not yet, anyway.

Behind him, he heard Livvy returning gunfire. Bullet for bullet. And he hoped Livvy would keep this SOB occupied while he got to Yvette.

Judson bolted from the cruiser again, staying low while he scurried toward Yvette. She still wasn't moving or speaking, but when he latched onto her arm, he saw her eyes open just a slit.

Alive.

For now, anyway. She wouldn't stay that way for long, though, with all that bleeding.

Even though it appeared the woman was seriously injured from a gunshot wound to the chest, Judson still took the time to make sure she wasn't armed. No signs of a weapon. Her hands were empty, and she didn't have a purse. However, she did have pockets in her jeans, and he patted them down while he dragged her to the cruiser and out of the line of fire.

The gunfire shifted, no longer being aimed at Livvy but rather coming at Judson. He didn't take the time to return fire. He just kept moving until he got Yvette to the side of the cruiser.

It was possible that just moving her had made her injuries worse. But he hadn't had a choice about that. Their attacker had fired at least two dozen shots, and many of them could have hit Yvette.

Hoisting Yvette up, he laid her on the back seat, and, staying low, Judson did another weapons check. But nothing. The keys were in the ignition, but the woman didn't even have a phone on her.

"The ambulance is on the way," Addie relayed to him.

Good. But whether it would make it there in time was anyone's guess. Added to that, the EMTs wouldn't be able to approach the scene until the threat from the gunman had been contained.

Judson decided to contain it.

He pulled out his backup gun from a slide holster and handed it to Addie. "If Yvette tries to hurt you, shoot to kill. Understand?"

Addie gave a shaky nod.

Since he could be leaving Addie with a killer, he hated

dumping all of this on her, but he didn't have a lot of options. Livvy couldn't get to their cruiser unless she took a major risk of being gunned down. Judson couldn't let that happen.

Readying his gun, he got out of the cruiser again, and in the same motion, he took aim over the roof. And straight toward those trees. Judson fired and fired and fired.

From the corner of his eye, he saw Livvy rejoin the attack after she reloaded, and she sent her own rounds in the direction of the shooter.

Finally, their attacker stopped firing.

And Judson had no doubts, none, that he or she was getting away. Unlike the attack at the ranch, though, he didn't go running in pursuit this time. He couldn't take that risk.

Not when it would be Addie's life he was putting in yet more danger.

He shoved aside the notion of catching the gunman and instead focused on getting the identity of the SOB from Yvette.

"Who shot you?" Judson demanded, getting right in the woman's face. "Who were you running from?"

Yvette stared up at him with eyes full of shock and pain. She opened her mouth, but nothing came out for what seemed to be an eternity.

"You have to stop him," the woman finally said. "He'll kill her." Yvette's words were all breath and had barely any sound.

Still, Judson heard her loud and clear. "Stop who?" he demanded.

She opened her mouth again, but this time, nothing came.

"Stop who?" he repeated, shouting the question at her.

But Judson was talking to a woman who couldn't answer. Her breath rasped in her throat, and her eyelids drifted down.

Yvette was dead.

Chapter Twelve

Addie sat at the dining room table at the ranch and read through the statement she'd just given Grace. A necessary statement in what was now another murder investigation, but Addie had hated going through it all over again.

Still, she would have gladly given the statement if she'd thought this would put an end to the danger. An end to the nightmares the attacks and abduction had caused. But it wouldn't.

No.

She knew the memories of seeing Yvette die would stay with her for the rest of her life.

"Thank you," Grace said when Addie did an e-signature on the laptop screen. The sheriff stood. "Is there anything I can get you? Other than Judson, that is?"

Despite everything, Addie managed a weak, short-lived smile. She did indeed need Judson, but because of those legal necessities, they had been placed in separate rooms of the house to be interviewed. Bennie had been tapped to take Judson's statement, and Addie knew that Grace would now be shifting rooms to take Livvy's.

"I want to see Judson and the twins," Addie muttered. In fact, at the moment that was all she wanted.

Grace nodded as if that was the exact answer she'd expected. “He should be in the kitchen.” But then she tipped her head to the front of Addie’s shirt. “I’ll need that first so the lab can analyze it. Let me grab an evidence bag from my cruiser.”

Addie glanced down and saw the blood. Not hers. But rather Yvette’s. It hadn’t come directly from Yvette, either, but from Judson, who’d transferred it to her when he’d pulled her into his arms shortly before the ambulance and backup from the county had arrived.

“I’ll be right back,” Grace said, heading to get that bag.

Addie went in search of Judson and found him where Grace had said he’d be, in the kitchen. And he was in the process of stripping off his clothes. She nearly whirled around to give him some privacy, but after everything that’d happened, privacy seemed like too low-level of a concern. So, she waited.

And watched.

It was hard to tear her gaze away from him as he took off everything but his boxers. More memories came.

Not of death and blood this time.

But of Judson and her together. Even now, it was impossible for her not to notice that he still had an amazing body. One that caused the heat and the old need to start simmering between them.

“I need his jeans and shirt,” Bennie said, his voice and expression filled with apologies. He held up an evidence bag and put the items in it when Judson handed them to him.

Judson kept his gaze pinned on her, searching her face to see how she was doing, while he fumbled around in his go-bag for the change of clothes.

“Grace needs my shirt, too,” she said, managing to get her throat unclamped. She didn’t know if that was because the emotion was catching up with her or because she was in the kitchen with a nearly naked Judson.

She decided it could be both, and once Judson was dressed and had pocketed his keys and phone and reholstered his weapons, Addie walked into the adjacent laundry room to grab a clean top. Since Etta Jean had been doing laundry when this whole abduction nightmare had started, several of Addie's shirts were already out of the dryer and folded.

"I'll step out for a minute," Bennie said, obviously getting out of the way so she could change.

Thankfully, Judson went into the laundry room with her. Thankfully, too, he didn't give her any privacy, because she didn't want him to. She wanted him right by her, and if seeing her without a shirt caused that heat and need to ripple again, then so be it. Addie didn't want him out of her sight.

She pulled off the top, taking a clean one off the top of the folded stack, and the moment she pulled it on, Addie stepped into his arms. Mercy, she needed this. She needed him, and Judson gave her that steadying comfort that no one else could. In the back of her mind, she knew she was falling hard for him all over again, but she couldn't stop it.

Correction: She didn't *want* to stop it.

He continued to hold her and brushed a kiss on the top of her head. Addie probably would have lifted her mouth to his to make it a real kiss, but the sound of footsteps stopped her. A moment later, Grace appeared in the doorway of the laundry room.

"Sorry," she muttered, holding up the evidence bag.

Addie stepped away from Judson so she could get the top and hand it to Grace. "What happens now?" Addie wanted to know.

"The clothes will go to the lab to see if there's any trace

or fibers to tell us where Yvette has been the past twenty-four hours," Grace explained. "That, in turn, could tell us if she had an accomplice."

"An accomplice," Addie repeated in a mutter. "You mean Trevor, Jennifer, Shane or Elijah." She stopped. "Well, maybe not Jennifer. When Yvette was running, she shouted out, 'You have to stop him. He'll kill her.'" Those words were still repeating like gunfire in Addie's mind. "If she was referring to Jennifer, then the *him* could have been one of the three men."

Grace nodded. Then shrugged. "Or Yvette could have been talking out of her head. Perhaps in shock."

Maybe, but that didn't feel right to Addie.

"It's also possible that Yvette was talking about someone she hired. The accomplice angle again," Grace tacked on to that. "Yvette could have hired someone to attack Judson and you here at the ranch. Then, the hired gun could have turned on her for some reason and killed her. Yvette could have been worried that this person might go after her daughter."

Addie tried to envision any of their suspects doing just that. And she decided any one of them could have. Of course, it was equally possible that Yvette had acted alone in the abduction and attack at the ranch. Still, someone had murdered her, and that someone had tried to do the same to Judson, Livvy and her.

"While you were giving your statements, Eden managed to get her hands on Yvette's will," Grace continued a moment later. "Apparently, she made a new one less than a week ago, and she left everything to her kids. She specifically stated that no one else was to inherit anything. That *no one else* included a husband."

Well, that was interesting, and it made Addie wonder

if Yvette had had her suspicions about her husband. Or had Yvette done this simply to try to repair her relationship with her daughter? Either way, Trevor wasn't going to care much for that.

"Who knew about the new will?" Judson asked.

"Not her family," Grace provided. "Well, not unless Yvette told them herself. The lawyer said the will had just been signed and processed and that he hadn't even given Yvette a copy of it yet."

Neither Shane, Jennifer, Trevor nor Elijah had mentioned the will, so it was possible Yvette had kept it to herself. But if she hadn't, if Shane and Jennifer knew about their inheritance, then it strengthened their motive for murdering her.

Grace had just finished bagging the shirt when both her phone and Judson's sounded with texts. They both looked to see what the message said.

"Group message from the CSIs," Grace relayed. "They're going over Yvette's car now, and they found something." She stopped, looked at Judson. "Apparently, a suicide note."

Of all the things Addie had thought the sheriff might say, that wasn't one of them. "Yvette was running for her life when we got to her," Addie pointed out. "Is the note real or something her killer planted?"

"We might soon find out," Grace murmured just as another text arrived.

Because Addie was still right next to Judson, she saw this message was a photo attachment. "The note," he said, holding his phone so they could both see it.

This wasn't some pristine, typed letter but something that appeared to have been hastily scrawled on a napkin from a fast-food place.

"'I'm so sorry,'" Addie read aloud. "'I can't live with what I've done.'"

That was it. Not even a signature. Definitely no last words for her kids. And that made Addie instantly suspicious.

"Yvette would have told Shane and Jennifer she loved them," Addie remarked, and she got immediate sounds of agreement from both Grace and Judson.

"So, either she was coerced into writing this, or she didn't get a chance to finish it," Judson concluded. He glanced up from the photo to meet Grace's gaze. "I got a look at Yvette's car, and it'd been run off the road. There were skids on the pavement from where it looked like she tried to stop."

"That was Livvy's impression, too," Grace said. "The person who shot Yvette could have maybe hoped to make her death look like a suicide. When that failed and when she started running and you guys showed up, the killer had to resort to shooting her. And trying to eliminate any witnesses by shooting Livvy and the two of you."

Yes, all of that was possible.

Grace opened her mouth to say something else, but the sound of raised voices stopped her. Judson automatically stepped in front of Addie, and he drew his gun. Grace did the same. Addie might have pushed them both aside to try to get to the babies, though, if Bennie hadn't stepped into view.

"Elijah, Shane, Trevor and Jennifer just arrived," Bennie let them know. "They're demanding to speak to you," he added before he hurried off. No doubt to make sure the visitors didn't barge in.

Grace sighed and looked back at Addie. "When I called to do the death notification, I told them to meet me at the station. I didn't want them here around you or the twins."

Addie got that. She didn't especially want the trio around the babies, either. But she did want to see something.

"Will you tell them about the will?" Addie asked Grace. "Because I'd like to see how they react to that."

The corner of Grace's mouth lifted into a smile. "Oh, yes, I'll definitely let them know, and I won't be having that conversation in the house but rather on the porch, so you'll both be able to watch and listen. The babies are tucked away safe with Etta Jean?" she asked.

Addie nodded, but she sent a text to Etta Jean to tell her to take the twins into the bathroom. Yes, she wanted to see the reactions to the will, but Addie didn't want that info to come with any additional risks to Lily and Rose.

"Do any of the four have alibis for the time of Yvette's shooting?" Judson asked Grace as they all made their way to the front of the house.

"Nope. I asked them that when I did the phone notification, and all claimed to be at home or on their way home. We'll check and see if that can be verified."

"I will see her now," Shane shouted, his voice so loud that it would have drowned out anything else that Grace said.

Elijah wasn't exactly being quiet, either. He was yelling out a demand to see Grace and Judson. Trevor was in the mix, too, shouting at the top of his lungs. Addie couldn't hear Jennifer at all.

When Judson, Grace and she made it to the front door, Addie saw Livvy and Bennie were blocking Shane and Elijah from coming in. She spotted Trevor on the porch steps, and Jennifer was by the gate. Jennifer was the only one of the four who looked grief-stricken, and it was obvious the woman had been crying.

"What the hell happened to my mother?" Shane demanded when his attention landed on Grace. The man also shot looks of disgust at Judson and Addie. "Did those two kill her?"

"Throttle back now," Grace snapped through clenched teeth. "Or I'll arrest you on the spot."

"Yeah, yeah, and kill me, too," Shane taunted. "Just like they murdered my mother."

"They didn't kill Yvette," Grace said, moving between Livvy and Bennie to face Shane head-on.

"Then, damn it, who did?" That came from Elijah. Like Shane, his face was tight with rage.

"We're looking into that." Grace aimed a warning finger at Elijah when he took a menacing step toward her. "If I have to arrest you for threatening a police office, trespassing and other assorted charges, it'll mean hauling you down to the station. It could be hours or days before you get any info from me. Or you could all just shut the hell up and I'll tell you right now what I know."

That silenced Trevor and Shane, but Elijah still looked ready to push Grace. He seemed to rethink that after sliding glances at the three other cops, who were clearly ready to back up their boss.

"All right," Grace continued once they'd all hushed. Well, their shouts and accusations had stopped, but Shane and Elijah were still doing some glaring. "Yvette was shot and killed by an unknown assailant. She appears to have been fleeing from that assailant when she died."

"Unknown assailant," Elijah snarled in a *yeah, right* tone. "You can't make me believe those two didn't want her dead because she took those kids." He turned his glare on Addie and Judson.

Grace shrugged. "Believe what you will, but they didn't kill her, and there's a manhunt for the person who did. To rule yourselves out as suspects, I'm asking you all to submit to GSR testing."

That brought on more cursing from Shane and Elijah, but Trevor stepped forward. "I'll do it," he said.

"So will I," Jennifer agreed.

Elijah tossed her a *what the hell* look, clearly not approving of her cooperation. If it was cooperation, that was. Jennifer could have still been the shooter, but maybe she was certain there wouldn't be any residue on her clothes.

"I want to know what happened to my mother," Jennifer added, showing some defiance of her own against Elijah. She shifted her attention to Judson and Addie. "Did she say anything before she died?"

Addie heard the question, but she focused on the reactions of the three male suspects. All of them seemed to have a second or two of stunned silence while they considered that.

Or feared that.

Were they worried that Yvette had said something to incriminate one of them? Maybe.

"She did say some things," Grace admitted. "We're going to analyze it further and try to enhance the dash-cam feed."

That sent Shane on a cursing spree. "What kind of doublespeak is that? Tell us what she said."

"Sorry, but I'm not at liberty to disclose that," Grace fired back. "But as soon as the analysis is done, I'll be in touch. Trust me on that."

It sounded like a threat, and while her expression, tone and badge had Elijah backing up a step, Shane held his ground.

"However, I can give you some other info," Grace went on a heartbeat later. "It's about Yvette's will." She paused, waiting until all four were staring at her. "Did any of you know that Yvette redid her will last week?"

Trevor groaned and muttered something under his breath that Addie didn't catch. "I told her not to give in to Shane's demands."

So, he'd known the change to the will was possible, and it made Addie wonder if Trevor had used those drugs to try to stop her. In fact, the drugs might come up if Trevor decided to challenge the will.

"Yvette left everything to her kids," Grace let Trevor know. "She purposely excluded anyone else, including a husband."

Elijah smiled. Actually smiled. Until he must have realized that wasn't an appropriate response and shut it down.

Trevor certainly wasn't smiling. He was riled to the bone, and, cursing, he stormed off the porch, headed to his car and then sped away.

Addie shifted her attention to Shane, who wasn't smiling but did appear more than a little shocked. It was the same for Jennifer, who began to cry again.

Elijah hurried off the porch to go to her, and he tried to put his arm around her, but she stepped away from him. The man didn't show any irritation over the rejection. Instead, he turned back to Grace.

"How soon will Shane and Jennifer be able to settle Yvette's estate and get the money?" he asked.

"Stop it, Elijah," Jennifer snapped before Grace could respond. Well, respond other than rolling her eyes and making a loud huff. "Just go wait in the truck for me," Jennifer ordered.

Now, the irritation came, but Elijah didn't push back. Probably because he figured out that badgering Jennifer wouldn't help him get his hands on her dead mother's money. Kicking at a rock that was on the pathway, Elijah went to the truck, slamming the door behind him after he got in.

"I did encourage my mother to cut Trevor out of the will," Shane admitted. "I still believe the man was solely after her money." He paused. "And I believe he could have been the one who killed her."

"Maybe," Grace said, not sounding at all convinced of that. "He agreed to the GSR test. What about you?"

The muscles tightened in Shane's jaw, but he finally nodded. "I'll be tested, too."

"Good. Then, go to the police station and one of the deputies will take the swab. The results come back like that." Grace snapped her fingers. "And you might be surprised at how hard it is to wash off gunshot residue. A shower and change of clothes usually aren't enough."

Shane stood in silence for a couple of seconds before he nodded and walked away, heading to his car. Jennifer, however, didn't budge. Not until her brother had driven away, and then she came up the porch steps toward them.

"Did, uh...are you sure someone killed my mother?" Jennifer asked. "Are you sure she didn't take her own life?"

Those questions seemed like giant, waving red flags, and none of them jumped to respond. Grace hadn't said a word about a suicide note being found in Yvette's car, but maybe Jennifer hadn't needed to be told.

Maybe she already knew.

"Did she take her own life?" Jennifer repeated. Her hands trembled while she wiped away more tears.

"Why do you think that?" Grace finally asked.

Jennifer didn't give a quick answer. She squeezed her eyes shut a moment, and a sob made its way from her throat.

"Because I think Mom was considering it. Ending things," she added in a hoarse whisper. "She was depressed. Or something. I think she was using drugs."

"Did she say that or did you see her use them?" Grace pressed.

Jennifer shook her head. "No, but something was off this past week or so. She left rambling messages about when she'd lost custody of Shane and me. In one of them, she said this place was evil, that the people here basically stole children from their loving parents."

Good grief. Addie had to bite back the anger and frustration over that. Yes, mistakes could and did happen in the foster system, but Mellie had worked hard for the children in her care.

"You didn't mention any of this during your interview," Grace reminded Jennifer. "Why not?"

For a second, Jennifer got the deer-caught-in-the-headlights look, but she shook it off. "I, uh, didn't remember until now." She paused and glanced around as if to make sure no one else was listening. "I think someone's trying to kill me," she whispered.

"Who?" Grace demanded.

"My brother, I think," she admitted after wiping away more tears. "I believe Mom told him about the change in the will. He was the one pushing for it. Him and Elijah," she added, her voice dropping to a whisper again.

"Has Shane done something specific to make you think he might want to kill you?" Grace asked.

Again, no quick answer, but Jennifer took out her phone and handed it to Grace. "I recorded Shane. And, no, I didn't tell him I was doing it, so I guess that's not exactly ethical."

"It's not," Grace agreed, but she took the phone. "What's on the recording?" she pressed.

"Just listen to it," Jennifer insisted. "And when you're done, maybe it'll be enough to arrest my brother for murder."

Chapter Thirteen

Judson sat in the makeshift office area that Addie and he had set up in her bedroom and checked to see if an update of Jennifer's recording had arrived on his laptop.

It hadn't.

But he knew something like that could take time. It wasn't just the accessing it from her phone but having the lab techs do thorough tests to make sure the recording didn't contain a virus.

And that it was real.

With all the advancements in AI, it was getting easier for people to do realistic fakes of such things, and Jennifer had a motive to do something like that. Well, she had motive if she wanted to cut her brother out of any inheritance from their mother, and a half a million was plenty of motive for her to want to do exactly that.

Since he didn't yet have the recording, Judson moved on to the latest report from the CSIs while he did some multitasking. He was keeping an eye on the twins, who were now asleep and listening for Addie in the shower. Thankfully, Addie was taking her time in the bathroom, and he hoped it was helping to ease her knotted muscles as it'd done for Judson when he had finally been able to wash off the remnants of Yvette's blood.

Now, listening to the water running and hearing her move around in there, he had tried not to think of Addie washing away blood. Tried not to think of her fighting the images of a woman being gunned down in front of her. Part of him wanted to go into the bathroom and try to soothe her. To check and see if she was all right.

But that would be playing with fire.

A naked Addie would be far too tempting, and an attempt at comfort might turn into full-blown sex. She didn't need that now.

Probably not, anyway.

And he admitted that wasn't a good thought to let stay in his head. He tried to shove it aside and focus on the report. Judson soon saw that it was dashcam footage not just from his cruiser but also the one Livvy had been driving when they'd come around that curve and seen Yvette.

Hell.

The camera had captured the woman dying.

Yeah, that was a way to yank his attention away from Addie and shower sex. It was the exact reminder he needed. They were in the middle of an intense murder investigation, and it needed his focus.

Judson watched the dash-cam feed frame by frame as it all played out again. Yvette running on the road toward them. The terror on her face as she begged for help. Help that hadn't come in time, because one of the slowed images showed the impact of the shot slamming into her body.

But another of the frames showed something else.

And that's what Judson zoomed in on now.

As that part of the road had just come into view, there was some movement in the trees to the right. Just a blur of motion, really, but judging from the location, it had almost certainly been Yvette's killer.

According to the memo attached to the report, the lab techs were in the process of trying to enhance the blur, trying to come up with any small detail that would help them identify who it was. Judson certainly couldn't tell from that smeared image, but he was hoping for something of a miracle. They needed to know who'd fired those shots so they could arrest him or her and put an end to the violence.

Judson swiveled around in his chair when he heard some movement in one of the bassinets, and he got up to check. Lily was wiggling and kicking her feet, but her eyes were still closed.

Still sleeping, well, like a baby.

It wasn't a surprise, since it was something that Addie had said the girls would do for at least another two hours. He was hoping Addie herself would do the same soon and get some rest or at least eat some of the sandwiches that Grace had had delivered from the diner in town.

He went back to his work area, sitting and using the keys on his laptop to freeze the screen on that blur.

On the killer.

And he played around with enlarging it and trying to change the colors and pixels enough to coax out some more details. He stopped again though when he heard Addie turn off the water in the shower. She didn't take long to dress because what seemed like less than a minute later, she came into the room wearing loose gray jogging pants and a black T-shirt.

Addie looked at him, their gazes connecting for a couple of heartbeats before she went to the bassinets to check on the babies. Then she turned, her attention settling on his laptop screen.

"What is that?" she asked, her eyes widening as she began to take it in. Addie headed straight toward him.

Judson sighed. Not that he could have kept this from her, but he'd hoped it could wait until the techs had managed to clean up the image. Maybe then he could have given her good news.

"It's the feed from the dashcams in the cruisers," he let her know and added, "You don't want to see this."

"Probably not," she murmured. "But I need to."

Hell. He debated if he could talk her out of this and decided the answer to that was no. So, Judson rewound it to the starting point of when he'd driven around the curve.

"Yvette," she said, leaning in closer to the monitor.

He made a sound of agreement, and before they got to the part where the woman was shot, he reversed the feed again and froze it on the shooter.

Again, Addie went even closer, studying it and no doubt doing what he'd done. Trying to figure out who the heck that was.

"The techs are trying to clean this up," he explained. "We might have something soon."

She seemed to latch on to that, and he saw some hope creep into her eyes. But that hope apparently wasn't going to get her to change her mind about continuing to view the footage where she would soon be seeing a woman murdered.

Judson was ready to let her take a look at all of it when his phone vibrated with a text. He'd shut off the sound so as not to wake the babies, but it still made a noise when it skittered on the surface of the desk.

"It's from Rory," he relayed to her. And then he saw the attachment. Not the dash-cam footage but something else that he'd been waiting for. "It's the recording that Jennifer gave Grace."

Judson welcomed the interruption and figured the recording wouldn't be nearly as gruesome as the dash-cam footage. At least he hoped it wasn't. But then, Jennifer had accused her brother of trying to murder her.

"The lab has authenticated it," he continued, reading through the info that Rory had sent along with the attachment. "It's real, and they've confirmed it's actually Jennifer and Shane speaking on the recording. The techs were able to do a voice analysis using the statements they both gave during their interviews."

"When did Jennifer record this?" Addie asked.

Judson found that in the notes, too. "According to the time stamp, it was one week ago today."

He adjusted the volume so it would be loud enough for them to hear but hopefully wouldn't carry to the bassinets. When he clicked the play function, he immediately heard Shane's voice.

"I repeat," Shane snarled. "We have to do something to snap Mom back to her senses. She's letting Trevor rule the roost, and if that continues, you and I are going to be flat broke."

"It's Mom's money," Jennifer replied.

"Yeah, but we're her kids, and if we don't do something and do it fast, Trevor will spend every last dime of it. If Mom was thinking straight, she'd want her own flesh and blood to have an inheritance."

Jennifer huffed. "She's got a blind spot when it comes to Trevor. She'll never choose us over him."

"She will if she has no choice," Shane spat out.

"What do you mean?" Jennifer asked after some hesitation.

"I mean, we have to do something. If she starts using again or drinking, then we can have her declared incompetent. We can take control of her estate. It'd be easy enough to tempt her into going back to her old ways. All I need is you to back me up. Us against Trevor."

Jennifer was silent for several seconds. "What are you saying, Shane? Are you planning on pushing Mom to use drugs or start drinking again?"

"It would only be temporary," Shane replied, as if he were certain that something like that would be reversible and not just flat-out wrong. Or dangerous if Yvette overdosed. "And then after we have her estate under our control, we can give Trevor the boot and get Mom into rehab. Once she's free of Trevor, she'll understand we did all of this for her."

"You're doing it for you," Jennifer snapped. "So you can get her money." She groaned. "I can't believe you'd consider drugging her."

"I didn't say I'd do it," Shane fired back. "But she could be…nudged in that direction. Maybe nudged into doing some other things that would help us get her declared incompetent."

"You are truly despicable." Jennifer added some harsh profanity to go along with that. "I won't help you ruin a woman so you can get her money, and if you try it, I'll tell her what's going on."

Now, it was Shane who cursed, and even though Judson's phone vibrated with another incoming text, he continued listening to the recording.

"Right, go whining to Mommy about me," Shane taunted. "You don't speak to her for weeks. You shove her away when her emotions catch up with her, and now you want to protect her. Do it," he stated like a threat. "And you'll be sorry. I'll come after you with both barrels and manage to convince Mom that you're lying. She'll believe me over you any day."

"I can make her see what you are," Jennifer said, but there wasn't a whole lot of conviction in her voice.

"Do that, *sis*." The word came out like the deadliest of venom. "Just remember, both barrels. I'm not going to let you get in the way of what I need to do to fix this mess she's gotten herself into."

With that, the recording ended, leaving Judson to wonder if it was truly the end of the conversation between the siblings or if Jennifer had only provided them with what she'd wanted them to hear.

The part that would incriminate her brother.

"This could be Jennifer's way of getting Shane out of the picture," Judson commented. "If he's locked away for his mother's murder, then he won't be able to inherit any of her estate."

He'd give that plenty more thought later, but for now he shifted his attention to the new text he'd gotten from Rory. Judson cursed after reading it. He had hoped this would be good news that could ultimately lead to an arrest.

"Rory got the results of the GSR tests," he explained. "Jennifer, Elijah and Shane all tested negative."

"And Trevor?" she asked.

Judson shook his head. "He didn't show up at the station. Grace is having him tracked down."

Blowing out a long breath, she sank down in the chair next to him. "You think he could be on the run?"

"Yes, if he's guilty," Judson replied.

That was a big *if*, though, because as far as Judson was concerned, it could be Jennifer, Shane or Elijah who was behind this. Hell, Elijah and Jennifer could be working together.

He saw the frustration and worry roll over Addie's face. She groaned, squeezing her eyes shut a moment. "I just need this to end," she muttered. "It eats away at me to think the babies are in danger."

Yeah, Judson was right there with her on that. They weren't his children, but, damn it, he loved them and he wanted them safe. Right now, it didn't feel they were close to making that happen.

When he saw Addie blinking back tears, he leaned over and put his arms around her. She didn't pull back. In fact, she moved out of her chair and onto his lap, pulling him into a hug as well. This felt right.

And wrong.

Addie was on an emotional edge. They both were. They certainly didn't have clear heads. But he didn't pull back, either, when Addie lowered her head and put her mouth on his.

Nope.

He just stayed put and let the heat do its thing. That soft kiss definitely packed a punch. Then again, just about everything Addie did had had a similar effect on him since they were teenagers.

"I know the timing is bad," she muttered with her mouth still against his. "But please, just go with it. Give us these minutes."

There'd been no need for her to add that *please*. No need for her to even justify what they were doing. Judson had been hot and ready from the moment this had started. And despite the timing, despite whether it was right or wrong, he was going to finish it.

He snapped her to him, letting the heat dictate the intensity of the kiss. And it was intense, all right. Scalding hot. Deep. French. It was also filled with plenty of that need that was building by the second.

She tasted good, like all the things he'd ever wanted in

his life. Like Addie. A taste that worked with the kiss and the body-to-body contact to amp up the inferno that was driving them both to find some release.

Judson wanted to slow things down. Wanted to take the time just to savor her. But that didn't happen. The kiss got even hotter. Even deeper. And Addie turned, moving until she was straddling him.

That shot the need straight through the roof.

Judson ditched the notion of slowing down, especially when Addie pressed her center to his. Especially when the kiss didn't stop. Especially when that need took on a raw urgency that made his body push toward getting her naked.

He didn't move her away from him, but Judson reached between them and somehow managed to locate the bottom of her shirt. Hard to do since she was in the process of trying to do the same to him. Still, he succeeded, stripping off the tee and the sports bra beneath, and with her breasts bare, he levered her up so he could take her nipple into his mouth.

She moaned, her voice silky and low, and she threw back her head, letting him taste her. Giving them both this moment while the hot storm continued to build and build.

Apparently, the building became too much for her, because she cursed him and went after his shirt again. Since she was clearly on a mission to remove their clothes, Judson decided to help with that.

It wasn't easy to shuck him out of his holster and shirt, but once his torso was bare, Addie returned the kissing favor by putting her mouth and tongue on his chest.

Judson heard himself groan. Felt the new surge of heat and need. Felt the urgency go up even more. He had to have her, and it had to be now.

He got up from the chair, sliding his hands around her

bottom to hold her in place while he carried her to the bed. Because she wrapped her arms and legs around him, they both landed on the mattress together.

And the kissing started all over again.

There was a frantic edge to it now. Hell, there was an edge to everything with the need heightened. With their bodies both pushing hard for release.

Judson peeled off her sweatpants. Then her panties. He couldn't resist dropping some kisses on her stomach. And lower. He got to hear Addie make another of those long moans, but she definitely didn't let him finish her off with his mouth. She clearly had a plan for the finishing, and that was for him to be inside her.

"Please tell me you have a condom," she said through gusts of her breath. She went after the zipper of his jeans.

"I do," he let her know. It was in his wallet, but it wasn't easy to get at it with Addie clearly on a mission to finish undressing him.

All the touching and wrestling around continued to hike up the need so by the time Judson located the condom, he was beyond ready. His jeans were suddenly the enemy, and he fought along with Addie to get them off. She didn't waste a second ridding him of his boxers as well.

"Now," she demanded.

He was right there with her, and the moment Judson managed to get the condom on, he rolled on top of her.

And into her.

The pleasure shot through him. Every inch of him. So hot, so strong that it robbed him of his breath. He didn't care. At the moment he didn't seem to need breath. He only needed Addie.

He pushed hard and deep into her as she lifted her hips, finding a primal rhythm that would help them find that release. Again, Judson tried to slow things down. Tried to hang on to each second of this. He managed it despite all the tight heat of her body that was trying to coax him into surrender.

Judson held on, kissing Addie again. Sliding his hand between them and touching her again. Building the need again and again. Until he felt the climax ripple through her. Until he saw the pleasure of release on her face.

It was perfect.

The right moment with the right woman.

With his body begging for its own release, Judson gave her one last kiss. And let himself go.

Chapter Fourteen

Addie was floating between waking up and a wonderful dream. Floating and experiencing a nice buzz from having sex with Judson.

Of course, this hadn't been their first time together. That first time had been awkward, fumbling, but still amazing. This latest one hit the amazing mark and then some without the other stuff.

Her body was practically still humming, and while part of her wanted to hang on to the dream, she decided to hang on to the man instead. She was hoping he not only had a second condom but that they could get in another round of sex before the babies woke.

She turned in the bed, her hand hoping to land on a still-naked Judson. But it didn't. And when she felt around the mattress and realized he wasn't there, her eyes flew open. Oh, God. Had something happened?

Since the only illumination was coming from a night-light clear across the room, it took her a couple of frantic moments to spot him. He was fully dressed in his jeans, boots and shirt and was sitting in the rocking chair feeding Rose from one of the premade formula bottles they'd stored in the room.

"I didn't hear her wake up," Addie blurted, throwing

back the covers and getting out of bed. Good grief. She must have slept hard not to hear the babies. She usually woke if one of them stirred even a little.

Judson smiled at her and gave her a long, lingering look with his gaze sliding over her body. That's when she realized she was bare naked. Considering the amazing sex they'd recently had, that shouldn't have alarmed her, but it didn't seem right to be in her birthday suit with one of the babies awake. Addie snatched her clothes up off the floor.

"Why didn't I hear you, or Rose, get up?" she muttered.

"Because you were getting some much-needed sleep," Judson was quick to say. "And besides, Rose didn't actually make much of a sound. I'm a light sleeper, and when I heard her moving around, I slipped out of bed, changed her diaper and got her a bottle. I've seen you feed the twins often enough that I know how to do it."

He did indeed know how, holding the tiny bottle at the correct angle, and Rose seemed perfectly content being in Judson's arms.

Addie glanced at the clock and was surprised to see that it was already after midnight. She had figured both babies would wake up sooner than this, since it was rare for them to go longer than four hours. Apparently, they'd needed their sleep as much as Addie had. That sleep for Lily was soon coming to an end, though, since the little girl was already beginning to wiggle.

Rather than wait until Lily broke into a cry, which she would almost certainly do any second now, Addie picked her up and kissed her. She took a few extra moments just holding her before she changed Lily's diaper and took out another bottle of formula. The timing was perfect, since Rose had just finished her feeding, and Judson stood to do the burping and uptime against his shoulder with the baby while Addie settled in the rocker with Lily.

This seemed odd. But normal, too. And she tried not to allow herself to slip into a fantasy of this being their usual routine. There were way too many unknowns for that, so she pushed this warm, fuzzy feeling aside.

"Did I miss anything else while I was asleep?" she asked. Though she figured if he had good news, he would have already told her.

"I've gotten a few texts," he admitted while he gently patted Rose's back. "I had to specifically ask Grace to send them to me, though. She was trying to give me some time to rest, but I wanted to be kept in the loop."

"So do I," she let him know. "I'm guessing from the way your jaw muscles are stirring that we still don't know who shot and killed Yvette."

"We don't," he verified.

Which meant the killer was still at large. And they weren't safe.

"You said that you just needed this danger to end," he reminded her. "But it might not happen any time soon. We might have to stick with these arrangements for a while."

Part of that suited her. The part with Judson being here with her and the twins. But Addie knew she couldn't live like this. If they didn't identify the killer soon and make an arrest, then she might have to ask Judson and Grace about setting up some kind of lure or trap to catch them.

"I saw a note on your nightstand," he went on a moment later. "It's a reminder for you to return a call to your adoption attorney."

Addie nodded. Then she sighed. "Yes, she tried to contact me yesterday when I was waiting to give my statement about Yvette's murder, but I let the call go to voicemail. I wasn't in the right frame of mind to talk to her," she settled for saying. "I listened to the voicemail, and it, uh, wasn't good."

Judson stopped walking and stared at her. "What do you mean?"

She gathered her breath and snuggled Lily just a little closer. "The lawyer wants me to hold off on the adoption petition until after the killer is caught and I can guarantee that the babies are safe. Added to that, she believes I should include a statement in my petition outlining future safety measure I'll take to make sure there's no repeat of what happened."

He continued to stare at her. "Will the abduction affect your application for adoption?"

Addie wanted to say no but couldn't. "Maybe," she admitted and then went with the truth. "Probably." She had to take a moment to tamp down the churning in her stomach over the possibility of not being able to become a mother to these babies. "There's no doubt others want them, and the adoption agency might consider them to be better parents than I can be."

"No one would be better than you," Judson was quick to assure her.

He believed that. And she hoped it was true. But Addie couldn't forget that they'd had sex just hours earlier and that might be playing into his assessment of her. Heck, their entire past together certainly colored his thoughts.

"The powers that be might not see it that way," she muttered.

Judson started walking again and stopped right in front of where she was sitting. "I'll marry you if you think that'll help your petition."

Addie's mouth dropped open, and while she was stunned,

she was pretty sure that Judson was, too. She was betting he hadn't given that a lot of thought before he'd thrown it out there like that.

"Marry," she repeated, and because she didn't know what else to say, she repeated it a couple more times.

"That proposal isn't about the sex," he spelled out before she could manage to say just that. "It's about Lily and Rose. And, I mean, it's not as if we don't know each other."

"So, it is partly about the sex," she said.

He looked ready to shrug and then seemed to remember he had a baby on his shoulder. A burping one. The sounds added a bit of lightness to the serious tone that'd settled over the room.

"All right," Judson conceded. "The sex plays into it. Things are…good between us in that department."

They were better than good. However, she could practically hear the *but* to follow that. Good sex was a start, but it shouldn't be the foundation for a marriage, one that included a ready-made family with preemie twins who were going to need a lot of care, love and attention.

"I appreciate that," she told him. And she voiced that *but.* "It's a bad time for either of us to be making big decisions about our future." Then she spelled out another issue. "And I don't want to tie you into a relationship for the sake of the babies. It's honorable, yes. Very honorable," she amended. "But if you're honest with yourself, you'll see it isn't what you really want."

She frowned and felt the stir of fresh emotions. Disappointment was leading the pack, followed closely by the dread that she'd just shut down something she shouldn't have.

Something she wanted.

She did want Judson. Addie wanted him, marriage.

Heck, a bright, rosy future together with their twin girls. But this wasn't a fantasy she could force or lure Judson into. If he truly proposed, she wanted it to be for the right reasons.

For love.

Judson opened his mouth to speak, and Addie held her breath. Then she heard the silent profanity in her head when his phone vibrated doing its little dance across the desk.

Talk about lousy timing, but when he walked to the desk, looked at the screen and muttered, "It's Grace," Addie knew the phone call could be more important than the personal stuff going on between them.

Because until this investigation was over and the killer was caught, any and all personal plans had to be on hold.

Judson eased Rose into her bassinet and took the call. Thankfully, he didn't step out of the room so she wouldn't be able to hear, but instead he moved closer to her and put the call on speaker.

"Addie's here with me and listening in," Judson let his boss know right off the bat.

Grace sighed. "I was hoping she'd be asleep."

"I slept some," Addie piped in.

"Good. We'll all need a long sleep once this ordeal is over," Grace replied. "And we might be closing in on that. Finally." Addie was ready to cheer or at least blow out a breath of relief, but then Grace added, "There might have been another murder, though."

Judson bit off the profanity that he started. "Who?"

"Possibly Trevor," Grace was quick to let them know. "After he didn't show for the GSR test, I had two reserve deputies go to the hotel where he was supposed to have been staying. When they arrived, the door was ajar so they entered, and they saw blood on the floor. But no sign of Trevor."

Addie had to stop herself from cursing, too. She wasn't a fan of Trevor, but if he'd been murdered, that meant the killer wasn't stopping.

But why?

It was beyond frustrating that they still didn't know the motive for these deaths, the two attacks on Judson and her, and now the blood found at the hotel. Heck, they didn't even know if Courtney's murder was connected to Yvette's. It could have been two different killers.

Or even a single killer working with a hired gun.

Shane, Jennifer and Elijah didn't have huge bank accounts, but Addie figured the money might not play into it. There were other ways to entice an accomplice.

Such as the babies.

It crushed her heart to think that someone wanted to get their hands on the twins so they could offer them up on the black market. If Yvette had had any part in setting that in motion, then Addie wished the woman a thousand deaths. She felt the same way about anyone else who had that as their motive.

"How much blood did the deputies find?" Judson asked, yanking Addie's attention back to the conversation.

"Nowhere near the amount found at the scene where Courtney was murdered," Grace answered.

So, maybe Trevor wasn't dead after all. And it was possible that it wasn't even his blood. Trevor could have been the attacker, and the blood could belong to someone else. Maybe that accomplice. Or even one of their other suspects.

"There's some spatter and maybe cast-off on the walls and floor," Grace continued a moment later. "That could indicate some kind of blunt-force trauma. And before you ask, the hotel didn't have any security cameras except in the lobby. The manager is handing over the feed to the techs as we speak, so they might be able to see Trevor and/or the killer coming and going."

Good. And Addie hoped that feed was better at capturing the image of the attacker than the cruisers' dash cams had been.

"What's the time frame for this possible attack?" Judson asked.

Grace's groan was a sound of pure frustration. "Anywhere from when Trevor stormed away from the ranch until about an hour ago, when the deputies found the blood."

Judson echoed that frustration. "I'm guessing Shane, Elijah and Jennifer don't have alibis?"

"They don't. I just had phone conversations with all three of them. Elijah and Jennifer can't even corroborate each other's whereabouts. Apparently, they haven't seen each other since they were at the police station doing the GSR test. Shane claims after he did the test, he went home to grieve his mother's death, saying, and I quote, 'I didn't want an audience for that.'"

So, plenty of time for any of them to have gone after Trevor. Or vice versa.

"Is there any evidence whatsoever that Trevor might have staged the attack?" Judson asked.

"Nothing direct," Grace supplied. "But there's also nothing to rule it out, either. There was some toppled furniture to make it appear there'd been a struggle. *Appear*," she emphasized. "But no one in the hotel heard any sounds of an altercation or anyone shouting for help. Those walls aren't exactly soundproof, so someone should have heard something."

Addie considered that a moment. If Shane, Jennifer or

Elijah had come to the hotel room door, Trevor might not have had the chance to call out before it was too late. One blow to the head could have possibly knocked him out and caused the blood loss. After that, Trevor could have been carried or led away from the scene.

Or walked away, if he'd staged this.

If he'd done that, then he was likely in the wind, and Addie thought the main reason he would do that was because he was the killer. But did that mean he was trying to evade capture? Or had he gone into hiding so he could plan another way of coming after them again?

"Now, to the good news," Grace announced. "Well, good for us, anyway."

Addie's hopes soared again, and she pushed aside that possibility of Trevor launching another attack. They needed a break in this investigation, and maybe this was it.

"The lab was able to come up with a partial fingerprint on one of the bags of drugs found in the nightstand at the Cateses' house, and it was enough to get a match," Grace explained. "The print belonged to a woman named Sienna Flanagan, age twenty-six, who…ta-da, is a friend of Jennifer's. They've known each other since elementary school, and Sienna has a record for drug possession. That's why her prints were in the system."

Judson blew out a long breath. "Have you had a chance to talk to Sienna or Jennifer about this yet?"

"Not Sienna, but when she didn't respond to attempts to contact her, I had an APB put out on her. And I got phone records to confirm that Jennifer and she had a conversation as recently as three days ago. Before that, they texted about once a month."

That seemed like a solid link. Despite what Jennifer had said on that recording with Shane, she'd possibly wanted to push her mother over the edge. Maybe so she could be declared mentally incompetent. Maybe just to get her to do something reckless that would get her killed or incarcerated. Going to her old friends for the drugs would have been the first step.

"As for Jennifer," Grace added, "SAPD is sending officers to her place now, but I spoke to her on the phone when I first got the results on that fingerprint. She denies everything and claims she's being set up, either by Shane or Trevor. She also told me that Sienna and Shane are friends, too, but there's no phone record of him contacting the woman. Of course, he could have used a burner or met with her face-to-face, but for now, I'm following the evidence."

"And that evidence points to Jennifer," Judson concluded. "She's got means, motive and opportunity for killing her mother."

Grace made a sound of agreement. "Maybe for killing Courtney if the social worker saw something incriminating when she went to the Cateses' house." Then, she stopped and sighed. "It's all wrapped up in a neat little package except for one thing. Jennifer couldn't have been the one who fired those shots at Addie and you at the ranch."

No, she couldn't have. Because Jennifer had been at the police station at the time of the attack.

"I'll look for phone links between Jennifer and Elijah during that time frame," Grace spelled out. "Or links between Jennifer, Shane or Trevor… Hold on a second. I've got an incoming call from SAPD."

Addie looked up at Judson to get his take on all of this, and she saw the doubt in his eyes. She was sure it was in her own eyes, too. Because even if Jennifer was the culprit, she wasn't in custody. And neither was the person who'd fired those shots at them. So, two people at large if Jennifer was behind this. Of course, if it was Trevor, Shane or Elijah, they could have been working solo.

"A possible problem," Grace said, coming back on the line. "Jennifer isn't at her apartment. But Trevor is." She paused only a moment. "Judson, he's dead."

Chapter Fifteen

Judson wished for a cup of strong coffee as he began to read through the report Grace had just sent him. His head was throbbing, and every muscle in his body was tight to the point of being painful. Still, he didn't want to risk waking Etta Jean, the twins or Bennie, who was sleeping somewhere in the house.

The people he wouldn't have to wake were Rory and the two ranch hands also standing guard, with Rory inside and the others patrolling the grounds. One glance at Addie, and he could add her to the list of those who weren't sleeping. She was sitting right next to him, reading the same as he was.

At least she was eating something—one of the sandwiches from the small fridge that had been moved into the room along with the baby stuff and other supplies. Etta Jean had made sure they had plenty of sandwiches, fruit and bottled water. Two Cokes as well, but they'd finished those off shortly after their phone conversation with Grace two hours earlier.

A call to let them know about Jennifer's impending arrest.

And Trevor's death.

Correction: his murder. The SAPD cops had determined

that from the sixteen stab wounds on the man's body. A staggering number of injuries for it to have been self-inflicted, and the medical examiner had apparently agreed. According to the first line of Grace's report, Trevor's death had been ruled a homicide.

The murder was in SAPD's jurisdiction, so they would be the primary investigators, but also according to the report, Grace would be looped in and apprised of any developments. Grace, in turn, would update all her deputies, since each and every one of them was involved in hunting down the person responsible for Yvette's murder.

It was possible—hell, it was even likely—that both law enforcement groups were looking for the same killer, but they wouldn't know that until they had more information.

And knew the whereabouts of their three surviving suspects.

That bad news was in the second part of Grace's report. Jennifer, Shane and Elijah weren't responding to any attempts to contact them, and none of them were home. Considering that it was nearly three in the morning, when most people would have been in bed, that wasn't good.

There was the possibility that one or more of them had met an end like Trevor's. The killer could be cleaning house, and that might involve murdering anyone who would link him or her to this string of crimes.

Unfortunately, that cleaning up could involve Addie and him.

Grace hadn't come out and said that in her report, but she had stated that Bennie and Rory would remain there at the Horseshoe Ranch until eight in the morning, when they'd be relieved by replacement deputies. Judson knew that meant their small-town police force was stretched well beyond the thin mark, and basically everyone was on duty until Jennifer was brought in and confessed. Or until they identified the person responsible, if it wasn't in fact Jennifer.

He would be eternally thankful to his fellow cops for diving into this with full force. That might be the very thing that managed to keep Addie and the babies out of harm's way. Of course, the only thing that would guarantee their safety would be for Grace to make that arrest and get the killer behind bars.

Judson ate some chips as he moved on to the second page of the report. This one was filled with the notes Grace had taken while the ME was examining Trevor's body at Jennifer's apartment.

Addie motioned to the part that had already caught Judson's attention. Trevor's head injury. Specifically, a fairly superficial cut and bruise that the ME hadn't believed would cause unconsciousness.

Or even any serious injury, for that matter.

Unlike the stab wounds, the ME stated that the angle of this one could suggest that it might have been self-inflicted. So, had Trevor tried to stage his own attack at the hotel and fled the scene, only to be attacked for real and murdered?

That was possibly how it had all played out, but it still left them with the huge question of why. If Trevor had been the accomplice to the person who'd murdered Yvette and even Courtney, that might make sense, but inflicting that many stab wounds was serious overkill. It implied the killer had been in a rage.

Or had the killer wanted them to think that?

Again, Judson had to go with a *maybe* here. The bottom line was they didn't know who they were dealing with, but these three murders were proof that someone would go to any and all lengths to accomplish their goal. Now, the challenge would be to discover the motive since that could lead them to the killer's identity.

"Why was Trevor at Jennifer's?" Addie asked, voicing the question that was repeating in his head. "And where's Jennifer?"

Judson didn't have an answer to either of those, only speculation. "They could have been working together. Or Trevor could have been lured there. And not necessarily by Jennifer."

"True," Addie muttered, and then she groaned and scrubbed her hands over her face. She also tried to stifle a yawn.

"You should try to get some sleep," he suggested. But it was more than a suggestion. Addie looked, and no doubt was, exhausted.

She looked at him. "I'll try if you will."

Addie leaned in and brushed her mouth over his. It was one of those barely there kisses that packed a solid punch. Then again, any contact with Addie always did that to him.

"I'll stand a better chance of getting some sleep if you're right there next to me," she muttered. With her mouth still hovering over his, she fluttered her hands toward the bed.

Hell. There it was again. That rush of heat and need. But Judson didn't think of sleep and rest when he glanced at the bed. He thought of sex, and while it would feel damn good to be with Addie like that again, he had to throttle back and stay focused. Not focused on her and great sex, either. But on trying to figure out the puzzle of this blasted investigation.

It took every ounce of his resolve to ease away from Addie. "I want to go back through all the reports again," Judson let her know. "Not just the ones that have come in tonight but those from the moment babies were taken. There might be something in them I've missed."

She nodded, and while the disappointment came through loud and clear, she straightened in the chair and pinned her attention to his laptop screen. "Then I'll go over the reports with you."

Judson sighed and then decided to play a little dirty. Not by kissing her, though that's what certain parts of him wanted to do.

No.

He played the baby card.

"Lily and Rose will probably be up soon, looking to be fed, and they might not go right back to sleep." He'd personally witnessed a few episodes of that when one or both of them would start crying and need some rocking and soothing. "You have to rest to be able to deal with that."

Of course, he would help if the babies were fussy and didn't settle. Heck, he'd help with just a routine feeding, but Judson was hoping that Addie would see the logic in at least one of them getting a little shut-eye.

And she did.

She stood and then did her own version of playing dirty by bending down and kissing him. This wasn't one of those pecks. It was long, deep and hot. And when she finally stepped away from him, they were both smiling. Both aroused, too. But Judson forced himself to stay put at the desk as she made her way to the bed.

Addie kept her gaze on him as she lay down and threw the quilt over her. He began rereading the reports, but he also volleyed some glances at her. Judson smiled again when he saw her eyelids drift closed. Maybe, just maybe, she'd be able to sleep without the nightmares taking over or any interruptions.

But that didn't happen.

She'd been asleep less than ten minutes when Judson's phone vibrated not with a text but a call. He muttered some profanity under his breath, but when he saw Rory's name on the screen, he got up, hurrying into the bathroom to answer it.

He didn't even manage to get the door shut before he heard Addie bolt out of the bed and make her way to join him. Since Addie was obviously awake and would insist on hearing what his fellow deputy had to say, Judson went ahead and took the call on speaker.

"We might have a problem," Rory said, and Judson heard the concern in his voice. "One of the hands, Calvin Hawkins, is patrolling near the front fence, and he says he saw a light in the barn across the road."

Hell. That was the spot where the sniper had set up for the first attack against Addie and him.

"I checked with the CSI head just to make sure it wasn't one of his guys returning to have another look around," Rory added a moment later. "And it's not. It's also not any of the other deputies. Of course, it could be some lookie-loo poking around where they shouldn't, but I wanted to give you a heads-up."

"What do you need us to do?" Judson asked.

"Just stay put for now..." Rory stopped. "Incoming text from Calvin." A second later, Rory cursed. "Take cover," he blurted. "Calvin says there's someone in the barn, and he's pretty sure the person has a rifle."

A RIFLE.

The words punched through Addie and had both her heart and her body racing back into the bedroom to get the babies. She had to get them to the bathroom before the shooter started firing.

Again.

It would be like the earlier attack. Bullets slamming into the house and possibly tearing through the walls. And just like before, the babies would be in grave danger. She had to protect them.

The girls were still sleeping, but she scooped up Lily anyway. Addie had reached into the bassinet to do the same to Rose just as there was a frantic knock on the door. That set Lily to start crying, and Judson hurried to the door to answer it. The moment it was open, Etta Jean rushed in.

"I heard Bennie say there could be a shooter in the barn," Etta Jean blurted. The panic and fear were evident in both her expression and her body language. She rushed to the second bassinet and gathered Rose up in her arms.

"There is," Addie confirmed. But she had to guess that the person was still getting in place since there hadn't been any shots fired yet.

"Rory and Calvin are moving closer to the barn," Judson let them know when he finished his call with Rory. "They both have rifles, too, and they'll see if they can get a visual on the person. And maybe take him or her out."

Addie prayed that Rory and Calvin could do just that. Eliminate the threat before any more shots were fired. But she also understood the necessity of them verifying who the heck this was. They couldn't risk killing someone who had simply been curious and was in that barn to poke around a crime scene. Still, it would be stupid of someone to do that, knowing that everyone on the ranch would be in a state of heightened alert.

"Let's get the babies into the bathroom," Addie insisted,

and after grabbing two bottles of the formula, she went in that direction with Lily.

Etta Jean was moving along right behind her, and, keeping a firm grip on Rose, she climbed into the bathtub. Despite the commotion and Lily's crying, Rose somehow stayed asleep.

"Hand Lily to me," Etta Jean insisted. She grabbed a clean towel from the rack, putting it on the surface of the tub like a pallet and easing Rose onto it to free up her hands.

Etta Jean had no doubt made that offer when she noticed Addie firing glances at Judson, who was still in the bedroom. He was on the phone again, probably getting an update from Rory, and she wanted to hear what the deputy had to say.

Addie went ahead and passed Lily to Etta Jean, and the woman immediately opened one of the bottles. The moment the nipple touched Lily's mouth, the baby latched on and the crying stopped. Addie hoped it stayed that way.

She hurried back into the bedroom with Judson and realized that he was still on the phone but no longer had the call on speaker. Addie moved right next to him, hoping to catch the gist of the conversation, but she could only hear murmurings on the other end of the line.

"I'll find some binoculars and have a look," Judson finally said, and then he added, "Stay safe," before he ended the call.

Judson put his phone back in his pocket, but before he could ask, Addie motioned toward the hall. "There are several pairs of binoculars on the top shelf of the foyer closet." Mellie had been an avid bird-watcher and had always kept extras on hand for any foster kids who'd taken an interest in that as well. "Bring me a pair. I want to try to see who's in that barn."

He frowned, and for a moment she thought he was going to refuse to do that last part, but he rushed off. Addie listened to the thuds of his running footsteps. She also heard the soft sounds Lily was making while she drank her bottle. What she thankfully still didn't hear were any gunshots.

She didn't like the notion of having weapons anywhere near the babies, but she wanted to be able to protect them. Addie went to her closet and took down the lockbox she'd stashed there. It, too, had been Mellie's, and Addie scrolled through the numbers on the lock to open it. She took out the loaded .38, and after making sure the safety was on, she went back into the bedroom.

Carrying two pairs of binoculars, Judson came rushing back in and caught a glimpse of the gun as she was slipping it into the pocket of her jogging pants. That deepened his frown even more.

"I don't want you in the line of fire," he was quick to point out, and he was adamant about it.

"Neither do I, but I want to be able to stop someone if they get past Rory and Calvin. Past Bennie and the other hand inside as well. You know full well there are too many ways in and out of this house, and a killer could slip past all of them."

He didn't dispute that. Couldn't, since he had personally used many of those ins and outs. It was an old Victoria house with side entrances and nearly two dozen ground-floor windows as well as the front and back doors.

"Try to stay out of the line of fire," Judson amended, and after he handed her a pair of binoculars, he crossed the room to the window that would give them a view of the barn.

Well, a partial view, anyway.

She wanted to curse when, after he pushed aside the

curtains, she could see there were some trees in the way. Judson ended up dropping onto his knees to try to get the right angle. Addie went to the floor with him, using the binoculars to peer over his shoulder.

Since there was thick clouds blocking the moon and sunrise was still hours away, it wasn't hard for her to spot the faint light coming from the loft area of the barn. She adjusted the binoculars, trying to zoom in, but the only thing Addie saw was that light, and it didn't seem to be moving.

"I'd rather you stay in the bathroom with Etta Jean and the babies," Judson grumbled. Like her, he was making some adjustments to his binoculars, trying to find a possible killer.

"I want to know who we're up against," Addie argued. "And whether it's one of our suspects or a hired henchman, I want to be ready."

Judson opened his mouth, probably to make another attempt to convince her to go into the bathroom, but he stopped and dropped down a few inches more. He kept his attention pinned to the barn.

"There you are, you bastard," he snarled.

"Where?" she couldn't ask fast enough.

"Not by the front of the hayloft. Look toward the back," Judson instructed.

Addie immediately shifted her aim, not onto the light itself but past it. And in the murky darkness she did indeed see something.

A person wearing all black, blending in with the night.

She leaned slightly to the side and saw something else. The light glinting off the barrel of what appeared to be a rifle. But neither the person in black nor the rifle was moving.

"What's he waiting for?" she murmured to herself.

Maybe he or she was trying to determine the best target. With Rory and Calvin out there, she prayed the attacker wouldn't just gun them down.

"I don't like this," Judson said under his breath. "If it's two of them working together, one could be coming closer to the house while we've all got our attention on this one."

Oh, God. Addie hadn't considered that, but it was a strong possibility. A two-pronged attack to take care of the protectors inside and outside the house.

Judson stood, taking hold of her arm and pulling her from the window. "I'm going up to the roof. I can climb through that old attic door to get there."

They were both very familiar with that spot. He'd climbed up there often as a kid just to look at the stars. Later on, when they were teenagers, she had joined him, and it had become one of their make-out spots. The roof had a panoramic view of the entire grounds.

And that barn.

It would also make Judson an easy target once he was up there. No place to duck and hide from a killer hell-bent on ending his life.

"I need to do this," he insisted.

Yes, he did. But that didn't make things easier. Addie had to force herself not to latch on to him and beg him to stay.

The kiss helped with that.

He lowered his mouth to hers, and along with robbing her of her breath, it nipped any objections she had in the bud.

"Go in the bathroom and stay put," he ordered, giving her one more kiss before he rushed out.

Addie stood there just a moment, trying to force aside the sickening feeling that it would be their last kiss. The last time she laid eyes on Judson.

No.

This couldn't be the last of anything but the danger. She refused to even consider a future without Judson, and she latched on to that thought—that hope—as she hurried toward the bathroom.

Addie had just reached for the doorknob when she heard the sound that she'd been dreading.

A gunshot.

Chapter Sixteen

Judson had just made it to the stairs when the gunshot blasted outside. And the sound punched him like a meaty fist.

Exactly where outside the sound had come from, he didn't know, but he didn't think the shot had hit the house. Still, he was ready to rush back to Addie's bedroom when his phone vibrated with a text.

From Addie.

Hell. His first thought was that Etta Jean, the babies or she had been hurt, and he had to tamp down the panic racing through him. He forced himself to look at his phone screen.

Are you all right? Addie had texted. We're okay here and staying down in the bathroom.

The relief shoved away the bulk of the panic, and he was able to reply with a thumbs-up emoji. A quick, way-too-light response that didn't convey the emotions he was feeling, but it got the job done. He let her know he hadn't been hurt, and now he knew that Addie, Etta Jean and the babies were safe.

Hopefully, they would stay that way if he managed to pinpoint the shooter and stop the attack from escalating.

That reminder got him moving even faster up the stairs to the second floor.

Another shot came.

His muscles turned to iron, and his heartbeat began to thunder in his ears. But again, this bullet hadn't seemed to hit the house, and it made him wonder if the gunman was aiming for Calvin or Rory. If so, he didn't want to text and possibly distract them when they were trying to stay alive.

Instead, Judson focused on getting to the center of the upstairs hallway and to the cord for the attic door. He gave it a hard yank, and the ladder unfolded as the door dropped open.

As he'd done countless times as a kid, he scrambled up the rungs, stepping into a massive space that was filled with an equally massive amount of stuff. Furniture that'd been able to fit through the door. Boxes, dozens and dozens of them, filled with all sorts of decorations for any occasion—birthdays, Christmas, Easter, swimming parties, homecoming and bon voyages.

Judson also knew there were thousands of photographs and old magazines, and he'd spent some time looking through those as a kid. The attic had become his sanctuary of sorts, and he was familiar with every inch of it.

Including the ceiling door that led to the roof.

Moving fast, that was where he headed.

It wasn't a standard feature in homes in this area, but he recalled Mellie saying that it had once led to a cupola. Apparently, storms had damaged the structure a century or more ago and it had been turned into a sort of widow's walk, a flat portion of the roof surrounded by a low rail. Over the years, the stairs had fallen down, but the ceiling door appeared to still be intact.

Judson was thankful for that since he needed to try to

pinpoint the location, and the identity, of this sick SOB who kept trying to kill them.

He heard another shot outside, but this one sounded as if it'd come from a different firearm. Or maybe just a different distance. He was hoping that meant Rory or Calvin had been able to return fire.

Pocketing the binoculars, Judson dragged a chair beneath the ceiling door, and, holstering his gun, he opened the door and used both hands and a good portion of his strength to hoist himself up. He immediately felt the chilly early-morning air close in around him, but he kept moving until he was on the widow's walk.

The moment he was through the ceiling door and on the walk, he drew his gun again.

The two-foot-tall railing around the widow's walk wouldn't give him much cover or protection, but it didn't obstruct his view, either. He could see nearly the entire ranch from this vantage point. Better yet, he could see the barn across the road.

Holding his gun in his right hand and the binoculars in his left, he zoomed in on the hayloft again.

And he cursed.

Because he could now see that it wasn't a person at all but rather what appeared to be a black jacket and pants pressed against some bales of hay. There was a rifle propped up beside it, and someone had positioned a flashlight so that it spotlighted the items.

Damn it.

There was only one reason for that setup—to make them focus on the very spot where the killer wasn't.

So, where was the SOB?

With his heart drumming faster now, Judson scanned the yard, the road and the pasture. He saw Calvin behind a sprawling oak. He had his gun, but he wasn't shooting. However, he had his attention pinned to the area across the driveway and in front of the house.

Judson swiveled in that direction, and he spotted Rory. His fellow deputy was crouched down by one of the cruisers, but he wasn't focusing where Calvin was. He seemed to be looking in the direction of one of the ditches.

Another shot rang out, blasting through the silence. And because Judson could see both Rory and Calvin, he knew the shot hadn't come from one of them. It had come from the gunman, and Judson thought he or she was in those trees across from the driveway. So, he turned there to keep watch, but he was well aware there could be two attackers.

One in each of the locations that had gotten Calvin's and Rory's attention.

If so, one of the attackers could be trying to get into the house while the other tried to pin Calvin and Rory down with gunfire. It was a plan that could work, and that's why Judson knew he had to give Bennie a heads-up.

Listen and keep watch for a possible break-in, Judson settled for saying.

Will do, Bennie immediately texted back. *You have a visual on the shooter?*

No visual, he replied. *Just an estimation based on that last shot. Also, there might be two of them.*

He imagined Bennie silently cursing when he read that. Cursing but staying vigilant. *I'm keeping watch,* Bennie assured him.

Judson was about to text Addie to give her the same warning and a reminder to stay put in the bathroom, but his phone vibrated with a text. Not from Bennie but rather Rory.

I think the SOB used the ditch to get closer to the

house, Rory had messaged. I caught a glimpse of him, but I don't think he's in the ditch now.

He? Judson questioned.

Or maybe she, Rory was quick to reply. I only got a glimpse of someone wearing all black. I shot at them, but I think I missed.

Too bad about that. Judson wished that Rory had blown this snake to smithereens.

Watch the house, Judson advised Rory.

And he did the same. Watched and waited. Listened.

The breeze didn't exactly cooperate with his attempts to listen. It came in short bursts, stirring the trees and rattling the shrubs and the leaves on the live oaks. Those little noises were maybe masking other sounds that he should be hearing. Like movement out of the ditch or that area across from the house.

What Judson wasn't hearing was any gunfire, but he wasn't exactly thankful for that at the moment. Of course, he didn't want any bullets going into the house, but if the SOB fired just one more single shot, that would help Judson pinpoint the location. Then he could return fire. Apparently, though, like the wind, the shooter wasn't going to cooperate.

Finally, after what seemed like a couple of lifetimes, Judson caught some movement from the corner of his eye. Not exactly in the area that Rory and he were watching. But rather to the right. At first he thought it could be the shrubs shaking from another gust of wind.

But no.

He spotted the shadowy figure as it darted out of sight. Judson got just a glimpse, and he couldn't tell if it was a man or woman. So, he continued to watch, taking aim in that direction. Readying himself in case he got the chance to put a stop to this.

More seconds passed, dragging by, and finally Judson caught another burst of movement. Someone wearing all black. Someone threading their way through the underbrush.

And toward the house.

He cursed himself for not having already hurried back downstairs so he could be waiting for this clown when he made it to the door.

But the person didn't run toward the door.

Judson shifted his gun, trying to lock his aim on the person, but he or she wasn't staying still. Nor were they moving in a straight line. They were weaving through the trees and bushes, using them as cover.

He pivoted again when he caught another glimpse. But the person darted behind one of the vehicles parked out front.

Judson moved, too, scrambling to edge of the widow's walk so he'd be in a better position to shoot. He was still taking aim when there was more movement. The shadowy figure raced to a tree.

Then another.

Judson fired. And missed. The bullet slammed into the tree just as the SOB raced out from the other side. Straight toward the side of the house.

His heart went straight to his knees when Judson heard the glass shattering. And he knew exactly what that meant. The killer had broken the window and was getting inside.

Hell.

Judson had to get to Addie and the babies *now*.

"OH, GOD," ADDIE MUTTERED.

She had no trouble hearing the sound of shattering glass

and thought it'd come from a window on the side of the house. What she hadn't heard was a gunshot, which meant the glass hadn't broken from gunfire.

But rather from someone using different means to gain access to the house.

The killer, no doubt.

He or she was breaking into the house and would be coming for her. That gave Addie a slam of emotions, with fear being right there at the top of the heap. The babies were right here, and a bullet aimed at her—or anyone else, for that matter—could miss and hurt them.

She had to stop that from happening.

The jolt of adrenaline would help with that. So would Mellie's gun. She wasn't a markswoman by any stretch of the imagination, but she could use the gun and go after the killer before he or she made it to this part of the house.

"Wait here," Addie told Etta Jean. "Stay as low in the tub as you can with the twins. That's your best protection."

And Addie had to pray that it would be enough. Thankfully, it was an old-fashioned cast-iron one that might stop any gunfire from getting to them.

Etta Jean had plenty of fear on her face, and she was shaking her head before Addie even finished. "You should wait in here, too. You should stay with us where you'll be safe."

Maybe. But she couldn't. Addie had to put a barrier between the twins and the killer, and if necessary, she'd do that with her own body.

"Bennie's in the bedroom," Addie reminded the woman. "And Judson will be here soon."

She had no doubts about that. Well, he would be arriving soon if he'd heard the window shattering. Or if he'd realized the killer was breaking into the house. If not, well…she didn't want to consider that right now. Addie only wanted to focus on stopping the monster who had put her babies in harm's way.

Addie brushed a quick kiss on the twins' cheeks. "I'll lock the door behind me," she added to Etta Jean.

And with that, she hurried out of the bathroom.

She did indeed lock the door, and Addie immediately glanced around to find Bennie. He was in the open doorway of her bedroom, and with his gun ready, he was peering into the hall. Or rather, he had been until he heard her behind him, and he threw her a quick look from over his shoulder.

Correction: a quick glare.

Addie could see that even though the only illumination in the room came from the twins' night-light and the light in the hall.

"You're supposed to stay in the bathroom," Bennie reminded her in a hoarse grumble.

That had indeed been the plan when Judson had left to hurry up to the roof. But that was when the attacker had still been outside. The broken window had changed everything.

"I have my gun," she replied. "And there's no window in the bathroom. The killer will have to get through us to get in there."

Bennie muttered some profanity, but he didn't order her back into the bathroom. He just continued to keep watch of the hall. "Rory thinks there could be two of them," Bennie whispered. "So, keep an eye on the windows in here."

Sweet heaven. She had already known that was a possibility, but it shook her to the core to hear Bennie spell it out. Rory and Calvin would also be aware there was a pair of attackers, and that probably meant they wouldn't be coming into the house to help. They were likely looking for the second one before he or she could get inside as well.

Since there could be two of them working together, did that mean this was Jennifer and Elijah? Or, heck, Jennifer and Shane?

Maybe.

But it could be none of them if they'd gone the route of hiring thugs to do their dirty work. That didn't make the situation any less dangerous. Just the opposite. Because they might not be dealing with amateurs but rather trained killers.

That thought was eating at her like acid, so she had to nudge it aside. Addie also had to tamp down her breathing so that she didn't risk hyperventilating.

Her heartbeat was a problem, too.

It was so loud in her ears that it was making it hard for her to hear, which was critical when it came to stopping someone trying to get in through the windows or approaching up the hall.

She kept a firm grip on her gun. Stayed vigilant. Listening. Waiting. She also calculated that it'd been less than two minutes since she'd first heard that sound of the breaking glass.

Not long.

But it felt like an eternity.

If Judson had heard the glass, too, he would have likely made his way off the roof by now and was racing through the attic to get to the ladder in the second-floor hall. So, Addie listened for his footsteps as well.

And she heard something.

After a few more seconds, there was a heavy thud above her. Maybe the sound of Judson dropping from that ladder to the floor. If so, he would have immediately broken into a run, which meant he'd be here in under a minute.

And that caused every muscle in her body to twist and knot.

Mercy. Judson could be running straight into the killer. In fact, the killer might be waiting in the shadows to gun Judson down. Then, he or she would have a clearer path to getting to her.

She was about to call out to Judson, to warn him, but as she opened her mouth, the night-light blinked off. So did the overhead light in the hall, plunging them into total darkness.

Oh, God.

The killer had done this.

Had somehow managed to cut the power. Which wouldn't have been hard to do, if he or she had gotten to the fuse box on the kitchen wall.

But then she remembered something. One of the ranch hands was supposed to be in the kitchen. Had the killer knocked him out? Or murdered him? She prayed not, but if he was capable of it, the hand would have probably called out to let them know there was immediate danger.

Once again, Addie had to try to level her breathing so she could stay focused and listen. And she soon heard something.

Footsteps.

Not someone running. These were slow, cautious steps. And they were coming straight for the bedroom. Maybe Judson.

Perhaps the killer.

Heck, it could be both of them, one coming from the front of the hall and the other from the back that fed off the kitchen. Without any illumination and no windows, the hall was pitch-black. Judson wouldn't be able to see the killer.

And vice versa.

Except maybe that wasn't true.

If the killer had made plans to cut the power, then he or she could have also brought along night vision goggles. Which meant the killer could see Judson and shoot him.

Addie couldn't stop herself from moving closer to Bennie and the door. She wanted to be able to help Judson if he needed it. She also wanted to stop the killer from claiming a fourth victim.

She had to shut out thoughts of Judson dying. Of him being hurt and bleeding out the way Yvette had done. She was trying to shut out everything but the sounds around her. The footsteps.

Yes, she could hear them. From the front of the hall. That would probably be Judson, making his way to them. Risking his life to try to protect them.

Addie could also hear the faint whimpering of one of the babies, and she prayed Lily and Rose weren't frightened, that they weren't picking up on all the danger around them. Also, if the whimpering turned to full-out cries, the killer would have no trouble pinpointing their location.

That got Addie moving even closer to the door, but she came to a dead stop at the sound of the gunshot. It roared through the house, a deafening blast that sent her heart racing and her fears skyrocketing.

Mercy.

Had Judson been shot?

She couldn't accept that. Wouldn't. And she tried to listen for any indication that he was hurt. But all she could hear now were those full-out cries from not just one baby but both of them. Probably from the sound of that gunshot. She hated that the little girls were being put through this.

Addie blinked several times, trying to get her eyes to adjust to the darkness, and she could finally see Bennie.

Well, the outline of him, anyway. She couldn't see anything or anyone in the hall, though. It was a black void where a killer no doubt was coming for them.

But where was Judson?

Was he lying in wait, too? Waiting until he could see the killer before he tried to take him out?

There was more movement. Footsteps this time. And she heard Bennie mutter something under his breath that she didn't catch. But she had no trouble catching the next sound.

Another gunshot.

This one seemed even louder than the first, something she hadn't thought possible. Maybe because it was closer? Was the killer right outside the bedroom door? It certainly seemed as if he was.

There was a flash of light. A bright burst of it, and Addie thought of those old cameras with the bulbs. It caused spots in her vision, smears and blurs blending with the darkness. It must have done the same for Bennie, because he rubbed at his eyes with the back of his left hand.

There was another shot.

Even louder, and closer, than the last one.

Bennie made a sound. A sort of grunt, and now that she could see slightly better, Addie saw something she definitely hadn't wanted to see.

The deputy collapsed in the doorway.

God, had Bennie been shot?

Addie couldn't see any blood, but it would have been next to impossible to catch sight of that anyway in the darkness and based on the way he'd fallen. Bennie was curled up in a heap on the floor.

However, she had no trouble seeing the figure that hurdled over Bennie. It happened at the exact second she heard another gunshot. But it wasn't coming from the figure wearing all black and night-vision goggles.

The shot had come from the hall.

Addie brought up her gun, trying to take aim.

But it was too late.

Everything was too late. The killer charged right at her, ramming into her and knocking her to the floor.

Chapter Seventeen

Judson couldn't see squat because of the blinding light that the SOB at the end of the hall had flashed at him. But his hearing was just fine, and he heard all sorts of sounds that had him charging forward despite not being able to see.

The babies were crying.

Then there'd been those gunshots. Followed by someone falling onto the floor. The thud had been unmistakable. But had it been Addie who'd fallen? Had she been shot?

"Addie," Judson managed to get out, and the thought of her being shot got him moving even faster.

But not fast enough.

Despite not being able to see much of anything, he cleared his eyes enough to catch a glimpse of a person jumping over something and into the bedroom.

Hell.

Where was Bennie?

Keeping his gun raised and moving closer to the doorway, Judson soon got the answer to that. Bennie was on the floor, and he was bleeding. Maybe dead. He certainly wasn't moving.

Judson had to shove aside the possibility that his fellow deputy might have been the killer's latest victim. He couldn't deal with that now. First, he had to somehow get

Addie, the twins and Etta Jean to safety and then capture the killer. Then he could get Bennie the medical help he needed.

He considered firing off a quick text to Rory, to let him know what was going on, but every second was precious now. Judson knew that in every bone in his body. He knew he had to get to Addie or this SOB would kill her.

If he hadn't already.

Judson made it to the door, stopping by the frame and getting another quick glimpse of Bennie. The man was breathing. That was something, at least. Maybe he could hang on a little while longer.

Maybe Addie could, too.

He peered around the edge of the door, hoping to see her—alive. And he did. But his heart dropped to his knees. She was definitely alive, for now anyway, but there was a person behind her. Someone wearing black clothes and night-vision goggles.

And that someone had a gun pointed at her head.

Damn it. The killer had her.

Now that his eyes had refocused from the burst of light, Judson took in the rest of the room with a sweeping glance. There was a small device on the floor that looked to be an attachment for a camera flash. It'd been simple but effective in temporarily blinding Judson. Heck, probably Bennie, too, which explained how the deputy had gotten shot. He wouldn't have seen the killer coming right at him.

Judson continued looking around and spotted another gun on the floor. Maybe the one Addie had had been using. The killer could have knocked it out of her hand when he'd come at her. So, she wasn't armed and couldn't defend herself without risking a fatal shot to the head.

He shifted his gaze from Addie to the bathroom door,

and Judson was glad to see that it was closed. Glad, too, that with the babies crying, he at least knew they were alive. He had to do something to keep them that way.

Had to do something to free Addie, too.

There was only the one person behind her. That didn't mean that someone else, an accomplice, wasn't outside the house. The killer's backup. And it sickened Judson to think that the accomplice might have killed Calvin and Rory. Maybe the ranch hand who'd been in the kitchen as well.

Judson heard some soft footsteps to his right, and he snapped his gaze in that direction. His body braced for an attack.

But it was Rory and Calvin.

Alive, and unlike Bennie, neither of them was injured. Thank God. And the fact they were here told him that this person was probably acting solo.

Judson motioned for Calvin and Rory to stop. He didn't want the killer hearing them and pulling the trigger in panic.

"What do you want with Addie?" Judson shouted out to the killer.

And he was certain this SOB wanted something or Addie would have already been dead. The only reason to hold her like this was for some kind of leverage.

"What I want is some cooperation," the man replied.

Judson cursed. He had no trouble recognizing the voice.

Elijah.

So, he was the killer. Maybe. Or he could be the accomplice. Still, even if he hadn't killed yet, he could be willing to start now.

"What I want is fast cooperation so we can all get the hell out of here," Elijah added a moment later.

The man didn't sound scared or on the verge of panic.

His hand wasn't shaking, either, and that let Judson know he was dealing with a cold-blooded killer. And it wasn't just Addie in danger. The babies were only a wall away from this snake.

"If you want fast, then spill why you're doing this," Judson snapped.

He stayed partially behind the doorframe so he could duck out of the line of fire if Elijah tried to shoot him. Which he was certain that Elijah would do—once he got what he wanted.

"Two things," Elijah said, still sounding plenty calm despite jabbing the barrel of his gun even harder against Addie.

It caused her to muffle a sound of pain, and while it was barely audible, it made Judson want to tear Elijah limb from limb. Which was no doubt why the man had done it. He likely wanted Judson on the edge, maybe going off half-cocked. That would make him easier to kill.

"First, take out your phone and toss it on the floor toward me," Elijah spelled out as he quickly yanked off the goggles. "I need to delete a picture."

Of all the things Judson had thought a killer might demand, that hadn't even been on his radar. "What picture?"

Elijah made a *yeah, right* sound as if he wasn't buying that Judson didn't know what he was talking about. Still, the man explained it.

"The one you snapped of Yvette's car as she was speeding away from the ranch. I was in the back seat with the brats, and I lifted my head just as I'm pretty sure you took that picture."

Yeah, Judson had no trouble recalling the photo. Or thinking that maybe he'd caught a glimpse of someone in the car with Yvette. But that glimpse had come a split second *after* he'd gotten the picture of the license plate. He had studied and restudied that photo, and there hadn't been even a partial image of anyone other than the driver in the car.

"Do it now," Elijah demanded, and he gave Addie another of those jabs to the temple.

Judson did take out his phone, and he considered hurling it at Elijah and trying to hit his hand. But it was too risky. It might distract him, yes. Might even cause him to drop the gun. But it also could cause him to accidently pull the trigger and kill Addie where she stood.

Instead, Judson leaned down, putting the phone on the floor on the other side of Bennie, and he shoved it in Elijah's direction. Since Elijah was standing in the middle of the room, the phone stopped a good yard short of Addie's feet.

Elijah cursed, and after calling Judson a crude name, he began to force Addie to move toward the phone. "I know the photo didn't go to the lab. I checked. I've got some decent hacking skills," he tacked on to that. "Of course, a county lab doesn't have as much cybersecurity as it should. I saw what was logged in, and the photo wasn't one of the items."

Elijah was right about that. The photo hadn't been sent in because the only thing of value on it was the license plate number. There'd been no glimpse of the back seat or anyone in it, only the trunk and the license plate.

Of course, Elijah wouldn't have known that.

All he would have seen was Judson aiming his phone at Yvette's car. If his image had indeed been captured, it was possible the lab techs could have cleaned up the image and used it to ID him.

So, yeah, in Elijah's mind, getting that picture was critical.

But once he had it, there'd be no reason to keep any of them alive. In fact, just the opposite. He'd want them all dead. Maybe Etta Jean, too, once he discovered her in the bathroom and realized she could have overheard everything they were saying.

"You helped Yvette steal the babies," Addie spat out. She was probably terrified, but she managed to sound more than ready and willing to make him pay for what he'd done.

"Helped?" Elijah laughed while he kept her moving. "Sugar, I did all the hard work by convincing that dimwit Yvette that the babies were in danger from some fake bogeyman I made up, and I made her believe that the only way to save them was for us to kidnap them. Yvette went right along with everything, including handing the brats off to the first person she saw on the road. Of course, she wanted to keep them, and I had to talk her out of that. Dimwit," he repeated in a snarl.

"I'm sure the drugs you gave Yvette helped convince her," Judson snarled. He wanted Elijah's attention on him.

"Maybe," Elijah muttered, and then amended that with, "Probably. They didn't hurt, anyway. They made her more pliable."

So, he'd been the one to give Yvette the drugs, which had made her more suspicious. What else had Elijah done?

"Why have her take the babies only to give them to someone else?" Judson wanted to know.

"The brats weren't the goal, *Deputy*." Elijah said the title as if it were the worst kind of poison. "Giving Yvette a motive to off herself was. After the drugs wore off and she came to what little senses she had, she was supposed to be so overcome with guilt that she couldn't live with herself. Of course, I would have encouraged her to do that."

That explained the note found in Yvette's car. Maybe the woman had written it on her own, but Judson suspected

Elijah had *helped* with that, too. It'd been why it was so impersonal.

"And the visits to see Rowena in jail?" Addie asked. "Did you *encourage* Yvette to do that?"

"I did," Elijah admitted. "I figured Rowena could stir up the old feelings for Yvette over losing custody of her kids."

"But why?" Addie pressed.

Elijah cursed, clearly growing more impatient, but he answered. "I needed that trail," he spat out. "After Yvette was dead and the cops started digging, I needed there to be some kind of reason why Yvette was spurred to take the kids. I figured the cops would think it was because of her conversations with Rowena. I didn't expect Shane to start going with her on those visits," he added in a grumble.

"What about Courtney?" Judson pressed just as Elijah got to the phone.

Hooking his arm around Addie's throat, Elijah reached down, and with Addie in tow, he snagged the phone and shoved it into her hand.

"Sugar, find that picture," Elijah ordered her. He gave her a third jab, no doubt to prod her to be quick about it.

Judson didn't want *quick*. He needed some time to try to figure out how to put an end to this jerk. And all the backup wouldn't help with that. In fact, backup could make things worse for Addie.

"Courtney," Judson repeated. "How does she fit into this?"

"She doesn't. She was collateral damage. A total accident, I swear," Elijah explained, his attention on Addie as Elijah tried to open Judson's phone. "What's your PIN?" he barked out to Judson.

Judson rattled off the four numbers. The real ones. Because while a false answer would buy him some time, it might set Elijah off. The man obviously had a short fuse on that vicious temper.

"Where was I?" Elijah muttered as Addie unlocked the phone.

"You were saying how Courtney's death was a total accident," Judson provided, and no way did he sound convinced of that.

"Oh, yeah. It was," Elijah insisted. "She was there at the house when Yvette and I got back. I was going to convince Yvette to take her own life and leave that suicide note. But that social worker was there, and she demanded to know if we took the babies. She was going to call the cops, so I had to stop her."

"But you didn't stop her," Judson pointed out. "She got away."

A flash of that quick temper darkened Elijah's face. "She did, but that was thanks to Yvette, who tried to hit me with a damn lamp. She gave me a hard knock on the head, and then she ran off, too. That's when I decided I'd have to find both of them and silence them for good. Courtney died on her own, bless her heart, but Yvette took a little more work."

"You gunned her down on the road," Judson spelled out.

Another shrug from Elijah, but he seemed to be getting more and more frustrated that Addie hadn't gotten to the picture he wanted. Since it was one of the last ones Judson had taken, it shouldn't have taken her long to find it, which meant Addie was stalling, too.

"And now with Yvette dead, Jennifer and Shane will inherit her money," Judson added, hoping to yank Elijah's attention back to him. "Were Shane and Jennifer in on it?"

"No, hell, no. Shane blabbered on and on about doing something to cut Trevor out of his mommy's life, but he's all talk. No way does he deserve a penny of that money.

And it'll be hard for him to collect with his sorry butt in a jail cell. There should be enough evidence to point to him murdering Trevor."

"But Shane didn't kill Trevor," Judson said. "You did."

"The man was in the way. He wanted justice for Yvette. Oh, boo-hoo," Elijah mocked. "So, now he'll help make me rich by being dead, and Shane will be going to jail for his murder."

Judson didn't know what evidence Elijah had planted, but he was sure the CSIs would find it when this was over. And he intended for this to be over with Addie alive and this SOB either under arrest or dead.

"There," Elijah said when Addie got to the picture. "Delete that and check for others taken from a slightly different angle. Then go to his sent folder to make sure he didn't forward them to anyone."

There had only been that one picture, and he hadn't sent it to anyone, but Judson was glad Elijah was searching for others. It bought him more time. Time he needed, because he still couldn't figure out how to get that gun away from Addie's head.

One possible move would be for Addie to drop down, to give Judson a clean shot to take out Elijah. That was a hell of a risk, but anything they did at this point was. Once she made it to the end of the photos and Elijah was certain there hadn't been any forwarded copies, he would kill them.

"You shouldn't have used the drug dealer with a connection to Jennifer," Judson threw out there, unsure if it would distract.

It did.

The man's head whipped up, and he got another flash of that anger. "I didn't know you'd be able to link that to her. I didn't know her friend's prints would be on the bag. And you shouldn't have harassed Jennifer for that." His voice got louder with each word. "I might have just broken into the house to get your phone, but I changed my mind because of way the two of you harassed her."

"We treated her like a suspect because she was found with blood on her hands at Yvette's house."

"She went there looking for Yvette," Elijah snapped. "Jennifer was in shock, and you damn near locked her up."

"You added to making her a suspect by buying those drugs from her friend," Judson pointed out just as fast.

Elijah cursed again, and it was raw and vicious. What he didn't do was take any responsibility for his fiancée nearly being arrested for murder. "I should kill all you idiot cops for going after her like that. Hell, I still might. Go faster through that sent folder," he snapped to Addie.

The man was quickly losing it, and that meant Judson only had seconds to stop him. Judson's gaze connected with Addie's, and he lowered his eyes, hoping she understood that he wanted her to drop down.

She gave a slight nod and stopped scrolling on his phone. "I took a picture of Yvette's car, too," Addie said.

It was a lie. Perhaps a very dangerous one. Because Elijah let out a loud roar, the rage tearing out in that feral sound.

"Where's your phone?" Elijah shouted, punctuating that demand with yet more profanity. He caught onto her hair and snapped her head back.

"It's in my purse in the foyer," Addie managed to say, though she was clearly in pain now.

But she was also clearly thinking straight.

As the last word left her mouth, she dropped, and even though Elijah still had hold of her hair, she fell far enough down that it gave Judson the opening he needed. He stepped into the doorway, and in one quick motion, he took aim.

And he pulled the trigger.

So did Elijah.

Both of them fired, but Judson's shot was a split second faster. Elijah's bullet slammed into the door next to Judson. Elijah, however, had no idea that he'd missed. The man had no idea of anything, not anymore.

Because Judson's shot hit Elijah right between the eyes.

The man was dead before he even hit the ground. And before he hit, Judson had already bolted across the room to Addie.

Chapter Eighteen

Addie lifted her face to the shower in the guest room and kept it there for as long as she could hold her breath. She had to wash away the blood.

Again.

This time, not from Yvette but from Elijah. When Judson had delivered the kill shots that had ended the man's reign of terror, and his life, Addie had gotten hit with some spatter.

It'd been a small price to pay for getting out of the nightmare alive, but she hadn't wanted the blood to stay on her body any longer than necessary. Nor had she wanted to hold the babies until she was clean. That's why she had headed to the shower as soon as Rory had bagged her clothes and taken a brief statement.

And after she'd spoken with Judson, of course.

That had been just quick reassurances that they were alive and unharmed. He hadn't kissed her and hadn't extended the hug he'd managed to give her right after shooting Elijah. That's because they had both wanted to rush into the bathroom and check on the babies.

Lily and Rose had been fine, not a scratch on them, and both girls had already gone back to sleep now that the gunfire had stopped. Etta Jean had looked just as shell-shocked as Addie no doubt had, but the woman was holding up. Addie prayed that continued in the aftermath of this attack.

The flurry of activity had started to swarm around the room and the ranch within minutes after Elijah's death. Priority one had been getting an ambulance for Bennie, but Addie knew that was just the start. The CSIs and ME would be coming in, and Grace and the deputies would be going through Elijah's place and any and all of his things.

Looking for proof to support what the man had confessed to when he'd been holding Addie at gunpoint.

Even if there was no proof, the confession and Elijah's actions in the past hour were more than enough to give him the label of serial killer, along with committing other assorted crimes, including the multiple attempts at the murder of police officers. Since Elijah was also the person responsible for abducting Lily and Rose and putting them in grave danger, Addie wouldn't shed a single tear over the man's demise.

Just the opposite.

Elijah's death brought her the flood of relief that the babies were now finally safe. They would be inconvenienced by having to leave the ranch for a day or two since it was now a crime scene. One that would need to be processed and cleaned up. That move would happen in an hour or two, after the deputies had cleared the grounds to make sure no other threat was lingering around. Everyone was convinced that Elijah had acted solo, but they wanted to be sure.

So did Addie.

She didn't want to take any chances with the twins' safety.

Then, the three of them and Etta Jean would be going to Judson's house for a couple of days. Not ideal, since it meant hauling loads and loads of baby stuff, but it was better than the alternative of being in the house where Elijah's blood was still on the floor. Soon, that would all be cleaned up, and while there would always be those horrible memories of him, there were thousands more good memories to overshadow what he'd tried to do.

Addie lathered up for a third time to make sure there were no traces of Elijah left on her body and wished it would be this easy to rid her mind of the terrifying images that would likely plague her for years to come. Etta Jean and Judson as well. Heck, the entire Renegade Canyon sheriff's office. Elijah had spread this nightmare to so many people.

And for what?

Money, plain and simple. His greed had spurred all of this, and she wondered if that greed would have soon extended to murdering Jennifer as well once he was certain he could have Yvette's entire estate.

Trying to shove aside as many thoughts of Elijah as she could, Addie stepped from the shower and was greeted by an amazing sight.

Judson.

He was in the doorway of the bathroom that she'd left open so she'd hear if anyone called out for her. Especially Etta Jean, since Livvy and she were in the nursery with the babies.

Judson's eyes locked with hers before his gaze slid down the naked length of her. The corner of his mouth lifted into a smile. Something she was glad to see. Right now, she wanted anything that would erase even a small portion of what she'd just been through.

He handed her a towel and watched as she coiled it around herself. "I would pull you into my arms right now, but that could be a little risky," Judson admitted. "I doubt we want to start something when we could be interrupted at any second."

That was true. But Addie risked it anyway. She went to him and let him engulf her in exactly what she needed. She let the feel of his body against hers ease some of her still-knotted muscles. Addie took in his scent, too, and let that fill her with something wonderful rather than the stench of gunfire and blood.

Yes, she needed this.

Addie held on for several minutes, letting herself level out.

"FYI, they just removed the body," he murmured, gently rubbing her back with his fingertips. "So, you won't have to see that when you go back downstairs."

Addie was beyond thankful for that. She never wanted to see Elijah again. She just wanted this moment with Judson and then the babies.

But she didn't get another moment with him, because his phone rang. Groaning, she stepped back, knowing he needed to take the call since it could be important.

"It's Serenity Springs Care Facility," he let her know.

He didn't put the call on speaker, and Addie didn't push him to do that. If this was Rowena, she didn't want to hear the woman's voice.

"Yes," Judson replied in response to what the caller had just said. "I'll tell her," he added a heartbeat later. "Thanks for letting us know."

Before he even ended the call, Addie knew what this was about. "Rowena's dead?"

He nodded, and she saw him studying her face, no doubt looking for any signs of grief. But there weren't any. Just the opposite. Addie exhaled a long, slow breath of relief and nodded.

"It's over," she muttered.

On a sigh, he reached for her again, but reaching was as far as he got before he got a text. Clearly, fate was not going to allow Judson and her a little alone time. Of course, that was expected with all the various wheels turning in the wrap-up of the investigation.

"From Grace," Judson relayed after looking at his screen. "It's a couple of updates. One about Bennie."

That grabbed her attention, and she steeled herself up in case the deputy had died, but she didn't see dread in Judson's eyes. Only relief.

"Bennie made it through surgery," Judson explained. "He's in stable condition. The doctor is optimistic that he'll make a full recovery."

That eased even more of her too-tight muscles. They had already gotten word that the ranch hand, Delbert Reeves, was doing well, too. He'd been in the kitchen when the lights had gone out, and Elijah had clubbed him with the butt of his gun. Delbert had needed stitches and would require a night's stay in the hospital for observation, but like Bennie, he would recover.

"Good," she managed to say. Elijah hadn't claimed another life. But Bennie, and the rest of them, were also going to have to live with the SOB's actions for a while.

"Grace also found out that Elijah had already managed to add his name on to Jennifer's bank accounts," Judson went on.

"How'd he do that?" she asked.

"Apparently, Elijah had her sign some online forms that Jennifer thought were for payments for her hospital bills from the miscarriage. But they weren't. They gave him full access to her funds."

So, that's how Elijah had intended to get his hands on her inheritance.

Judson looked at her again. Then he picked up the clean clothes she'd put on the vanity. "Want to go see the babies?" he asked. "They're awake. At least they were about ten minutes ago."

"Yes," she couldn't say fast enough.

Addie practically yanked on the jeans, T-shirt and slip-on shoes and started out of the bathroom the moment she was dressed. Her hair was dripping wet, but she didn't care. She wanted to hold the babies now and let them soothe her as only they could.

Since the guest room was on the second floor, they made their way to the stairs, past the attic ladder that was still pulled down. Before they even made it to the landing, Addie heard the chatter of the cops and the CSIs.

Once again, her house was crammed with first responders, and she hoped this was the last time such things would be needed. The only cop she wanted filling her home on a permanent basis was Judson.

That thought gave her a mental pause, and she tested out the idea of it again. Yes, she wanted that. She didn't want to lose this moment-to-moment contact, this intimacy, with him again. She stopped on the stairs, looking up at him since he was on the step above her.

"What?" he asked, at first frowning, but that faded fast. Maybe because he saw that need for him in her eyes. Yep, he saw it all right, because he smiled.

She smiled back, but Addie still didn't tell him what she was thinking. What she wanted.

What she needed.

Now wasn't the time for her to spill any of that to Judson. But soon. After she held the twins.

When they made it to the foyer, Addie heard yet another familiar voice, but this time it wasn't one she'd expected to hear. She spotted Grace in the front doorway, talking to Jennifer.

Addie could see the woman had been crying. In fact, she still was. She was swiping at tears as she muttered something to Grace. However, Jennifer's head whipped up, her gaze zooming right to the two of them.

Addie steeled herself, figuring that Jennifer was going to blame them for her fiancé's death. Heck, she might not even believe that Elijah was a killer, so things might get ugly in a hurry. Judson must have thought the same thing, because he stepped in front of her.

Protecting her, again.

Part of Addie thoroughly appreciated that, but she stepped to his side to face Jennifer. If the woman wanted to verbally blast them, Addie would tell her exactly how close Elijah had come to killing them.

But there was no verbal blast.

"I'm sorry," Jennifer said. "So very sorry."

"Jennifer heard about the incident on the news," Grace explained. "She's on her way to the police station to give another statement, but she wanted to stop by here first. I told her she couldn't go inside."

"It's okay," Jennifer quickly said. "I, uh, don't want to go in."

She shivered as if she could imagine the body and the blood of a man she loved. Or had once loved, anyway.

"I swear I didn't know what Elijah was doing. I didn't know he'd killed my mother, Courtney and Trevor." Jennifer stopped and pressed her fingers to her trembling lips. "I mean, I knew he wanted the money. He was always going on and on about that, but I didn't know he would kill to get it. And those babies. He tricked my mother into taking those precious little babies."

Apparently, that had made it to the news reports, too, or else Grace had mentioned it to her. Clearly, that revelation had shaken Jennifer to the core.

"I've also told Jennifer that she'll likely be cleared of all charges," Grace explained. "Unless, of course, we find something at Elijah's place or on his computer."

"I had no part in this sick plan," Jennifer insisted, frantically shaking her head. "So, if you find anything, it'll be something he set up to make me look guilty."

Judging from what Elijah had said when he was holding Addie at gunpoint, there'd be nothing to implicate Jennifer. Only Shane because he wanted Trevor away from his mother, maybe even dead. And the CSIs and cops would no doubt be able to sort that out.

"I won't keep you," Jennifer said, turning her attention back to Addie and Judson, "but I wanted you to know that I won't be keeping the money from my mother's estate. It doesn't feel right for me to have it when it was my fiancé who's responsible for so much pain. So much hurt." She swallowed hard. "I'll see a lawyer about donating it to the Horseshoe Ranch. Maybe as some kind of scholarship fund for the kids who are fostered here."

That touched Addie. The ranch was self-sufficient, but donations were always welcome. "Thank you," she managed to say around the lump in her throat.

Jennifer nodded and murmured another, "I'm so sorry," before she turned and walked away.

"If Shane shows, I'll send him straight to the police station," Grace said after Jennifer was in her car. "I figure he won't be nearly as tearful as his sister."

Probably not, but at least he was alive and wasn't in jail

because Elijah had framed him for murder. Once that sank in, Shane might be plenty thankful for the outcome.

"We'll be in the nursery if you need us," Judson said, and taking Addie's hand, they headed in that direction. Not taking a direct route, since that would have led them past the room where Elijah had died. Instead, they went out through the side porch to get to the kitchen and the back hall. The moment they reached the door, Addie heard an amazing sound.

Cooing.

She went straight in and saw Etta Jean sitting on the floor with the babies, who were lying on a quilt. Both Lily and Rose were indeed awake, and as Addie approached, they both looked up at her.

Twin smiles.

And no way would she believe that was gas. They were as glad to see her as she was to see them.

Addie dropped down on the floor next to them, giving them both kisses, which brought on yet more cooing. The tears came. Happy ones, of course, and she saw that Etta Jean had them, too.

She gave the woman's hand a squeeze. "We can watch them for a while so you can take a break."

Etta Jean nodded. "I do want to pack some things to take to Judson's." She looked at him as she got up from the floor. "Thank you for letting us all stay there."

"Anytime," he assured the woman, and he pulled her into a quick hug. "We'll leave as soon as Grace gives us the okay."

Another nod from Etta Jean, and she blew out what sounded like a breath of relief. They all needed to get away from the chaos for a while, but Addie was already looking forward to coming back home. To things returning to normal.

Well, her new normal, anyway.

Addie wanted some things to stay exactly the same. But she wanted some changes, too. For now, though, she just savored this moment. Her babies were smiling and making those wonderful sounds, and Judson was right by her side.

"I'll call my lawyer in a couple of hours and ask her to try to expedite the adoption petition," Addie told him. Now that the killer was no longer a threat and there wasn't any next of kin to try to claim them, there shouldn't be any obstacle standing in her way.

Judson smiled and sat down beside her. "Good. The sooner, the better."

She felt the same way. Lily and Rose were a huge part of that new normal. In a couple of months, she wanted to resume taking in foster kids, too, so the legacy of the Horseshoe Ranch could continue.

"Does the sooner, the better work for other things?" Judson asked.

Addie had been playing with Lily's toes, but she turned to stare at him. He wasn't quite smiling now, but there was certainly no gloomy expression on his incredible face. Just the opposite.

And his expression got a whole lot better—hers as well—when he leaned in and kissed her.

Oh, there it was. That dreamy feel of pleasure sliding right through her. The man could perform magic with that mouth.

He upped the magic by slipping his right arm around her and pulling her to him to add a hug to that kiss. It was plenty hot. But fun, too, because both babies were kicking them.

Laughing, Judson eased back from the kiss and gave both Lily and Rose a nuzzle on their cheeks. The girls clearly liked that, because they cooed some more.

"Well?" he said. "Does the sooner work for other things?" he repeated.

Addie hoped he was talking about their future, but just in case he wasn't, she went ahead and launched into things she needed to say to him. "I've been in love with you for a long time, Judson. Then we made that stupid pact. Not so stupid then, but it would be for us to try to hang on to it now."

Mercy, she was babbling. And she was nervous. Or at least she was until Judson smiled again.

"You're in love with me," he stated.

She nodded. Waited. Waited some more. Then his smile widened.

"Same," he finally said. "I've been in love with you forever, and that pact has dissolved to dust."

Addie would have smiled or cheered, but he kissed her again, and that pretty much robbed her of the ability to make any sounds or facial gestures. The kiss went on for several incredible moments before he eased back and gently nipped her bottom lip with his teeth.

"I'd love to haul you off to bed to celebrate," he said, "but I like this celebration just as much. Well, almost as much," Judson added with a chuckle.

"We'll do the bed celebration soon." Which hopefully wouldn't be too long. "For now, there's just one more thing I need to do."

She kissed him, and she made it way too hot, considering they had an audience of twin babies. Still, Addie had wanted this dizzying intensity from the kiss to give her the courage for what was to come. If Judson rejected her...but she stopped. Nope. She wouldn't go there. She would just spill and let him decide what to do.

"Will you marry me?" she asked. But she pressed a finger to his mouth to stop him from answering just yet. "And FYI, I'm not talking about a marriage of convenience or one simply for the sake of the twins. I'm talking the real deal, an honest-to-goodness marriage—"

"Yes," he blurted. And she caught just a glimpse of the grin he flashed before he hauled her back to him and kissed her as if to seal the deal.

Addie sealed it right back. She melted against him, savoring the moment. Savoring, too, the thought that she wanted many more moments just like this one.

Cooing, kicking babies. A really amazing kiss. And the man she loved. Her future husband.

Yes, this was exactly the new normal that Addie wanted.

* * * * *